The Way Back

Sophie Tate

Acknowledgements

Thank you to all my favourite people

x

Andy

Andy

1

*

'Can I take your name please?' The moody police officer asks looking down on me. He is towering over me and it's intimidating. His eyes are digging into me, questioning my innocence. It's making me feel guilty, even though I haven't done anything wrong.

'It's Andy,' I say after hesitating for a few seconds. He's making me so nervous that I'm having to think about my own name. He's acting so cold towards me and I'm helping, I dread to think how he treats the people who are actually committing crimes.

'And are you over the age of 18 Andy?' The second officer asks using my name as if it's an insult. My eyes shift over to him. He's much shorter, but not any happier than his partner. I wouldn't be able to tell which one plays *'good cop'*.

'I'm 20,' I confirm, desperate to get all these formalities out of the way. I'm sick of waiting, I want answers and I want to see her.

I impatiently watch as the short officer starts writing in his notepad. What could he possibly be writing down that is taking this long? Every few seconds, he looks up at me as if he's studying my appearance and writing it down. I feel myself getting impatient. Are they going to tell me something useful? Something I don't already know? If things were different and I wasn't in complete panic about Gracie, I would laugh at how small his notebook is. Instead, I stare at the top of his head. He is starting to go bald and the artificial lights are reflecting off his skin. I wonder how old he is, he looks too young to be losing his hair already. I look up towards the taller officer and he's glaring at me. I give him a weak smile but when he doesn't respond I look away and focus my attention onto something else. The rest of the room is in chaos. I guess in a hospital waiting room, everyone is having a crisis, it's not just my life that has been completely turned upside down today.

'So, can you tell me what happened?' The short officer asks, finally looking up. I sigh trying to hide my irritation. This will be the third time today that I have had to tell this story. I'm starting to get sick of telling it. I just want to see her now. I don't know why this is taking so long.

'I was walking home from work...' I begin.

It was raining and starting to get dark. I was standing at my front door trying to find my keys in my pocket. The pockets on my jeans were tight and I was struggling to pull them out.

'Is this number 21?' A small voice behind me asked.

Andy

'Yes,' I replied, 'this is my house, who is it that you're looking for?' I sighed, expecting to turn around and see some cold caller of some sort.

'I don't know,' the voice shook, grabbing my attention instantly and sending a shiver down my spine. I turned around slowly and there she was, just standing right in front of me.

'Gracie?' I whispered in shock. It was her, with her deep brown eyes and long, brown, knotted curls. Even after two years, I recognised her straight away. Her skin was so pale and so lifeless. My eyes widened in shock. I never thought I'd see her again. I couldn't help but just stare at her, it was like I was frozen on the spot. I didn't know what else to do. I was scared that if I took my eyes off her, she'd disappear again. And she just stood there, staring through me. It was like I wasn't even there. Her eyes were all fogged up and her whole body was shaking, rocking backwards and forwards. Then suddenly her body, just kind of slumped forward and hit the floor.

'HELP!' I screamed finally finding my voice and repeating it until someone could hear me.

My mum rushed out of the front door and ran towards us. At first, she just saw a body, I didn't have enough time to warn her that it was Gracie. She flinched when she realised, turning on her feet and running back into the house.

8

'I'm going to call for help,' she shouted. 'Andy, bring her inside.'

My mum went into survival mode and all my panic would let me do is follow her instructions. I scooped Gracie up in my arms. Her body was so light, it made me realise how much weight she must've lost in the past two years. I ran with her into the house. When I got into the living room, I put her on the sofa and looked for my mum. She was in the kitchen, already on the phone. I looked over at Gracie lying there and my brain finally kicked in. I rushed over to her and tried to wake her up, she wasn't responding to me at all. Her hair was completely soaked and her lips were starting to turn blue. Her skin was frozen. I knew she needed warming up, so I removed some of her wet clothes and replaced them with blankets. Then all I could do was to wait for help to arrive.

The police officers stare at me, nodding in unison as I finish my story. The short one is still writing in his tiny notebook. The tall officer squints down at me.

'Did you see anyone else in the area? Before or after?' He asks.

'I didn't see anyone,' I explain, trying to think back. If anyone was there, I don't think I would've noticed. I was too shocked seeing Gracie. 'Why? Do you think someone brought her here?' I question, wondering if there are any leads that they are not telling me about. When

Andy

Gracie went missing two years ago, I felt like no one was telling me anything.

'She was weak, I doubt she would have been able to walk very far on her own. That's why it's so important if you saw anyone.' The short officer explains, stressing the importance to me as if that's going to help me remember. I wish I had seen something, at least then we'd be closer to knowing what happened to her. When she first disappeared, they had nothing, no leads, no witnesses or anything.

'It was dark, there may have been someone there, but I didn't see anyone,' I explain wishing that I had anything that could help. The police officer looks at his co-worker and raises his eyebrows, sending some kind of secret message to him. I try to hide my irritation, they shouldn't be here questioning me, they should be out there looking for whoever it was who took her.

'That's all the questions we have for now. We just have a few questions for your mum. Thanks.' He places his tiny notebook into his inside pocket, nods and then they both walk away from me. I feel slightly relieved as they walk away, when she went missing the police pointed fingers at me first. I know in cases like this they always check the boyfriend, but I hated that they even suspected that I had done anything to hurt Gracie.

I watch as they slowly approach my mum, whispering to each other as they walk. My mum is sitting down on one of those cold and metal hospital waiting room chairs. I gave up sitting on them in the first twenty minutes of us being here. She is on the phone to her best friend Connor, Gracie's dad. He is working away in Dubai at the moment, currently being told that his daughter, who went missing nearly two years ago, is back. I can't imagine that being a fun phone call to make.

'Is her father here yet?' I turn to see one of the doctors who was here when Gracie arrived at the hospital.

'No, we have only just been able to get a hold of him, he's in Dubai so it will take him a while to get here,' I explain as the doctor starts to beep.

He looks down, distracted by his phone for a second before looking up and hesitating. He sighs and lowers his voice, 'look, we're only supposed to let family in, but considering the situation,' he pauses for a second, 'you can go in and see her. She's stable but a bit groggy, so be patient with her.' I feel the smile grow on my face, I thought I was going to have to wait for Connor to get here before I saw her.

'Ok, thank you,' I say gratefully, nodding to let him know I that I understand. He gives me a friendly tap on the shoulder before walking away. I almost feel bad, I kicked off big time at him and the other doctors earlier when they said I couldn't see her. I've been dying to go in since she arrived, even if she was just sleeping.

I look towards the room she's in and then over at my mum. She's speaking to the police officers now; I can already tell that conversation is going to take ages. There is no way I am waiting for her to finish. Besides, I want to see Gracie alone. For the past two years, every day I would think about seeing her again. In all those fantasies, I never imagined my mum being there when I was finally reunited with my girlfriend.

I see her lying on the bed and I suddenly feel really nervous and lightheaded, this all seems so unreal. They gave her a private room, for her safety and the other patient's too, I guess. She's been gone for so long, who knows what she has been through or what she's going to be like when she wakes up. It makes me feel sick when I think about all the places she could've been.

She doesn't notice me at first, so I stand there for a few seconds trying to think of all the things I have wanted to say. My head is in a complete mess; seeing her is a relief, but it's kind of bringing back the feelings of when she went missing. It tore me apart and I don't think I have ever been the same since. I try to swallow that feeling, there's no point in feeling it now that she's back.

Gracie stands in front of me looking down at me. I reach out to try and pull her down onto my lap. She laughs, taking a step back and dodging my arms. I feel a smile grow on my face; her laugh is contagious.

'Stop it,' she warns playfully.

'What, I'm not doing anything,' I say putting my hands up.

'You know what you're doing,' she laughs.

'Stay here with me tonight, please,' I almost beg. I've only just gotten her back; I don't want her to leave now.

'Not tonight, but tomorrow?' She offers.

'What about every night?' I respond and she shakes her head playfully.

'I'm sure your mum would love that!' She laughs.

'She'd just have to get used to it,' I laugh lying back down on the bed and pulling her on top of me. Before she can make any more excuses, I roll on top of her and kiss her. 'I love you,' I whisper quietly.

'I love you,' she replies and I feel my stomach starting to do cartwheels. After breaking up, I never thought I'd hear her say those words again. 'Now let me go and I promise I'll come back,' she whispers.

'You better keep that promise,' I tease, letting her go.

'I always do,' she pouts.

That was the last time I saw her. Those final moments have lingered in my brain ever since. If she had just stayed with me that night, then none of it would've happened. My biggest regret is not making her stay. I remember it so clearly, she had been avoiding me for weeks, ignoring my text messages, she would even leave her house when I would come over. It was killing me. The worst part was that there was no reason for it, like a switch she'd turn on and off at completely random times. When I was finally done with her, she would reel me back in. It was a vicious cycle that I was constantly stuck in and it went on for months. That night, she came back to me and it felt different like she wasn't going to change her mind again. She told me how sorry she was, that she didn't know what had gotten into her. It wasn't just me that she felt distant with, it was everything. I honestly thought that everything was finally going to be ok, until I woke up the next day to find out she was gone. When she told me that things were going to be different, I didn't think it would be like that.

'Gracie,' I say quietly, breaking out of my thoughts and peering into her room.

'Where am I?' She instantly turns to look at me. Her abruptness startles me, but I quickly get over that and smile. Everything seems the same, so normal, the way she looks, the way she speaks.

'You're in the hospital,' I say softly, trying to keep my voice calm. I walk slowly over to the chair by her bed. She watches me in silence as I sit down. 'Gracie, where have you been?' I ask, desperate to know the answer. I

need to know that she was ok, to calm all of the thoughts
that have been haunting me. She stares at me and I wait for
her to answer. She's silent for a few seconds, it's as if she's
thinking about her answer.

'Am I hurt?' She asks completely disregarding my
question. Her voice is so plain, I can't tell what she's
thinking, how she's feeling or anything.

'We don't think so,' I say, feeling caught off guard
by how blunt she is being with me, I don't know what I
was expecting but it wasn't this, 'they're just running some
tests to make sure that you aren't'. I smile at her to try and
reassure her; everything feels so awkward right now.

'Why do you need to make sure?' She asks slowly.
What does she mean? For the past two years we have had
no idea where she's been, of course we need to make sure
she's ok. I try to hide my irritation. I need to be patient like
the doctor said.

'You've been missing for two years,' I explain,
does she not realise that? 'Where were you?' I try again,
fighting my frustration. I really am trying to be
understanding, I know she has just woken up in hospital,
but I need more from her. It's been two years; I was her
boyfriend. She hasn't even acknowledged that it's me sat in
front of her.

'I don't know,' she says shaking her head.

'What!' I snap without realising. I know it's
selfish, but I can't help it. It's me sat in front of her and

she's treating me like a stranger. I'm trying not to feel angry but it's frustrating that after two years of pain and missing her, she is acting as if I am nothing. Even the way she's staring at me, blankly and completely unfazed that it's me sat here with her. Does she even care? Did she miss me? There's no emotion there at all, it's as if it's no big deal to her. It's like she's completely forgotten about what we had, it's as if... Then it hits me, 'Gracie, do you know who I am?' I ask.

'I don't know you,' her eyes flick away from me onto the floor, she just brushed that comment off her shoulder like it was nothing. She sounds so uninterested and she seems so unaffected by her words, the words that are hitting me right where it hurts.

'What!' I shout, unable to control my voice. After all this time, she doesn't remember me. Anger takes over my confusion. I stand up so quickly that the chair behind me hits the floor. It falls too quickly for me to catch it and the metal hits the floor. Gracie looks startled and I try to apologise to her, but the words don't come. Everything after happens so quickly, two nurses run into the room and behind them are the two police officers. Before I can do or say anything else, they grab me by my arms and try to pull me out of the room. I try to fight back and get free from them. I'm not finished, I still have questions and so much more I need to say to her. They push me out of the room and shove me onto the floor. When I stand up and turn back to them, my mum appears in between us.

'Andy!' She warns, the look in her eyes is enough for me to back down.

'If he doesn't calm down, then we will have to arrest him,' one of the police officers warn. He speaks over me as if I am a child. I take a step back and fall back onto the chair behind me and put my head in my hands. Everything happened so quickly, I'm not even sure what happened. All I know is that she doesn't know who I am, hot tears fall into the palms of my hand. I feel my mum's hand on my shoulder and look up.

'She doesn't remember me,' I say, finally catching my breath. 'She's back but she's not here.'

Andy

2

*

After two days, they finally discharge Gracie from hospital. It was killing me that they were keeping her for that long, I have been dying to see her again and they weren't letting me after my little episode. It was a complete misunderstanding, but they wouldn't listen to me. So I've been living vicariously through my mum and Connor's visits but apparently, she still hasn't really said much to them either. It sounds bad, but I'm relieved it isn't just me that she can't remember.

They've ran every test under the sun and they still can't find anything wrong with her. They suspect that the memory loss could have been caused by the trauma of wherever she's been, something about a coping mechanism. It breaks my heart to think that it's been that bad that her brain is forcing her to forget, but then if it is just a coping mechanism then surely, well I'm hoping her memory will eventually come back. I'm no doctor, but that seems plausible to me.

The whole thing is so mysterious and no one has any answers, not even Gracie. They are no closer to finding out who took her than they were two years ago. Even though she's back, we're still nowhere nearer to having any answers. It all feels helpless, I am just hoping that taking her home will help her get at least some of her memory back.

Connor and my mum decided the best thing to do was to have her stay in our spare room when she was released from the hospital. Connor didn't want to take her home straight away; he said his house wasn't ready, but I think he was scared. I don't blame him, especially with Gracie's mum being gone. It's his first time being a dad without her mum. I know he's struggling; he's still freaked out about having to tell her that the mum she doesn't remember, is dead.

Of course, my mum was more than happy to have them both stay. Gracie in the spare room and Connor on the sofa downstairs. It's been weird, Gracie and my mum never really had the best relationship, but Connor is her best friend, so she's really trying to help. I can't complain either, last night it felt good to have her so close to me, just down the hallway.

This morning, Connor and my mum left early to go and sort his house out for Gracie, leaving me to watch her. I have been dying to see her alone since being kicked out of that hospital room. I want to see her, speak to her and try everything I can to get her to remember me. So, like the complete loser I am, I have been standing outside the spare room waiting for her wake up.

'Oh, uh. Hi Gracie,' I say awkwardly when she finally resurfaces. I don't know why I feel so startled when she opens the door, I have literally been waiting here for her to do exactly that. She looks surprised when she sees me. I panic, trying to force more words out of my mouth. I must look like a right freak just standing here. 'I was just checking if you were awake.' The words clumsily fall out of my mouth.

'I'm awake,' she says simply, smiling at me. She looks happy to see me, surely that's gotta be a good sign? My eyes scan her. She looks a lot better, like she's back to normal, if there even is a normal for her now. She's wearing shorts and a vest top, it's slightly cropped, revealing a little bit of her pale skin. My eyes slowly move down to her legs and I force myself to look away, I don't want to make her feel uncomfortable.

'I was going to make some breakfast and I wanted to know if you wanted some?' I offer feeling awkward and hoping that's a good enough excuse as to why I am standing here waiting outside her door.

'Uh, yea,' she says, 'let me get ready and I'll meet you downstairs,' she suggests with a smile. I nod and silence follows. I hate how awkward it feels between us, it's weird. After a few painful seconds she turns around to go back into the room. Without thinking about it, I reach out and grab her hand.

'Uh Gracie,' I mumble, she turns around and looks at me expectantly. I panic, I hadn't thought that far ahead. Every word feels impossible especially when her big brown eyes are staring up at me like that. 'Do you remember?' I stutter feeling pathetic, I immediately look down at her hand in mine. I know asking her isn't going to change anything, but I can't help it. I am desperate for her to remember something.

'No Andy,' she says with a quiet voice. I don't want to believe it.

'You really don't remember **us**?' I ask feeling hurt and finally looking up at her. I know it's selfish, it's not just us she has forgotten, but how could she forget?

'No,' her eyes are doing everything they can to avoid mine. I just need her to look at me, to see me right now. This is stupid and I don't even know why I am trying but I'm desperate for her to remember something, even if it's small.

'Me and you?' I whisper, moving closer to her, she's magnetic. She finally looks up at me, into my eyes and something clicks. I still feel everything for her, maybe even more now. Nothing has changed for me. I can see something in her eyes, there's still something here. I know she still feels the same, she has to, she just doesn't remember it. She is so close to me now. I take a breath, to try and control my thoughts. I know this isn't the time to be thinking about her in this way, it's inappropriate. I should give her some space and take a step back, but it feels too good to be this close to her. I glance down at her lips; we're close enough to kiss. I think about it for a second, about kissing her. It would be wrong, so unfair. I can't, at least not yet.

I know I need to say something else now, but I can't think. Her just standing this close to me has wiped all the thoughts out of my brain. Ok. Words. Use them. All I can think about is how she is letting me this close to her. If she didn't like it, she'd move away? I can't think like that, that's not consent. I should just give her space, it's too soon for this.

And then she leans forward, even closer to me. Her face becomes a blur and she kisses me. **She** kisses me. Her. I freeze when I feel her lips touch mine. Should I kiss her back? Would that be wrong?

In a moment of weakness, all of my morals leave my body. I pull her closer to me, holding her face in my hands. She doesn't stop, instead she raises her arms and places them around my neck. Everything suddenly feels normal again. I fall back into a routine and slowly lower my arms down her body. I gently push her back against the wall and my body against hers. I feel her grip tighten around my neck and then I kiss her harder.

For a moment, everything feels normal again. But then, that moment ends.

'I'm sorry,' Gracie says pulling away from me. When she looks up at me, I see the sadness in her and I suddenly feel awful for putting her in this situation.

'It's ok,' I whisper. My heart is pounding. I instantly feel guilty for letting this happen. She's only been back for a few days, she can't remember anything, what was I thinking?

'It just felt right,' she says apologetically. I try to hide my smile, so I was right, there is something still there for her.

'You really don't need to be sorry,' I say backing away from her. 'I'll see you downstairs.'

I sit and wait for her on the sofa in the living room trying to calm myself down. The last few minutes replay in my head. My lips are buzzing and I can't wipe the smile off my face. She kissed me, she started it. That must mean that she still feels something for me, even if she doesn't remember. She wanted to kiss me. Why? She must still have those feelings somewhere. Although, I can't let myself get my hopes up, but I think it's already too late.

I sit up as soon as I hear her footsteps coming down the stairs. I stand up and walk to the bottom of the stairs to wait for her. I'm really trying to wipe the smile off my face, I don't want to freak her out by smiling like a crazy person.

'You look nice,' I say as she reaches the bottom of the stairs. She is wearing black leggings and a red jumper; red has always looked so good on her. She has her hair tied back showing off her beautiful face. My eyes follow her body and I find myself checking her out. Again, I need to push those thoughts away. I feel bad thinking like that, it's so wrong but in my head, she is still mine.

'Thanks,' she replies. The tone in her voice is so blunt and it catches me off guard.

'Mum and Connor have gone shopping,' I tell her, trying to break the tension that has just appeared and carry on the conversation as we walk into the kitchen. She follows me but says nothing. I feel like I am talking to a brick wall. She's looking around the room, her eyes are focused on her surroundings. She seems more interested in the wall than she is with me. There's something about her that has shifted. I just don't know what. Is she mad at me? She just seems a lot more closed off now. I don't even think she's listening to me. I watch her and wait for her to acknowledge what I am saying.

'Orange juice? Tea?' I ask finally breaking the silence and giving up on getting a response for the last thing I said. She looks up at me for what feels like the first time since she came downstairs. She looks offended as if I'm interrupting something and pauses for a second. I stare at her and wait for a reply. She stays quiet for so long that I start to question myself and what I said. It wasn't a difficult question, was it?

'I don't like orange juice, but I'll have a tea,' she says flatly.

'Two sugars,' we both say in unison. I laugh at the coincidence but stop when her eyes jump onto mine. She glares at me and I feel like sinking into the floor. I don't get it; she's acting completely different all of a sudden.

'I must have made you hundreds of cups of tea,' I say trying to lighten the mood.

'Hundreds, wow!' She says sarcastically, but I ignore it.

'We were in a relationship for nearly three years, that adds up to a lot of tea,' I explain walking around the breakfast bar to get closer to her. I don't know what has suddenly gotten into her, but I want to get back to how we were upstairs 10 minutes ago. I reach out and take her hand. She seems hesitant but doesn't move away. Then she looks up at me with those big, brown eyes again and this time I lean down towards her. I very slowly and gently put my hand under her chin and lift her head up towards mine. She gave me a dose of her earlier and it wasn't enough, I need more.

When she looks up at me, I feel it again, the moment. I lean in slowly. Towards her lips. I almost get there when she clears her throat loudly and completely disregards the moment. I pull away quickly and immediately make more space between us. My cheeks are on fire. Her eyes dart away from mine awkwardly and I suddenly feel bad for trying. I should've been happy enough with the first kiss and not have pushed for a second. I shouldn't be moving so quickly with her, it's not fair.

'So, what do you want?' I ask, trying to quickly recover from her rejection and change the subject to anything else. 'For breakfast I mean.'

'I'll have a dippy egg,' she says after a few seconds.

'Dippy eggs,' I repeat. That's what she used to call them before. I smile and try not to get too excited that she remembers that. I look over at her and she's glaring at me again. I clear my throat and try to hide my smile. I am no stranger to one of Gracie's bad moods, I'm just baffled as to how it came on so quickly.

3

*

'Gracie, I am telling you, if you don't give it to me now, I will come and get it from you,' I warn her.

'Oh really?' She giggles holding up my Xbox controller.

'I'm serious, you just interrupted a very important game,' I tell her.

'More important than me?' She pouts holding the controller to her chest. I stand up and walk towards her, she screams and jumps onto my bed. I chase her and she manages to dodge me and get to my bedroom door. Before she can open it, I push on the door.

'Now you're trapped, give it back,' I say holding my hand out.

'Make me,' she says softly and I feel my cheeks redden. 'You forgot to say please,' she sticks her tongue out at me. I gently push her against the door and hold her arms up in the air. She struggles but I manage to pull the controller from her hands and chuck it on the bed behind me.

'I think you're the one who forgot her manners when you snatched it out of my hand,' I say holding both her wrists in one of my hands.

Andy

'Now let me go,' she pouts.

'Say please,' I say. She giggles furiously and I lean in slowly, picking her up and throwing her down onto the bed, her laugh roars as I jump down next to her.

'Andy,' I look up to see Gracie standing at the kitchen door, staring at me.

'Gracie, you're awake,' I reply dragging myself back into reality. I smile at her cautiously, wondering what kind of mood she's in, I don't want a repeat of yesterday. She's staring at me through tired eyes; she looks exhausted, like she's barely slept. I can't tell whether or not she's happy to see me.

'And you're here,' she says, a smile spreads across her face and I feel relieved. I was worried that I had already fucked it up. I play it cool; I don't want things to go weird again.

After our awkward breakfast yesterday, Connor came back and brought Gracie here, to his house to settle in. I didn't want her to go but I knew it was the first step into getting back to normal. So, for the rest of the day I gave her space. I thought that it would be for the best, to let her get used to being back and also after our kiss yesterday I wanted to give her a chance to think about it. The last thing I want is to make her feel uncomfortable and after the way she acted while we were having breakfast, it made me realise that we need to take things a lot slower. She needs a friendship right now, so I am going to be the best, best friend she's ever had. So, when I woke up this morning, I decided to come straight over to see her and get started on this friend thing. Although, all I have done so far is sit here on my own and wait for her to wake up. Connor has been working in his office, he looked busy, so I've been trying my best not to bother him.

'I took a few days off work, so we could spend some time together,' I explain. Work didn't really have a choice, they had to be understanding in this situation.

'Good,' she says simply as she shuffles through the kitchen and towards the fridge. I look down at her feet to see she's wearing the most ridiculous pair of slippers. I'm surprised she can even walk in them; her feet are completely drowning in them. For a few seconds she disappears behind the fridge door. I start playing back the last few seconds in my head, did she look happy to see me? My mind starts to think up questions to ask her when she appears again, holding a carton of orange juice.

She starts searching through the kitchen cupboards, looking for something. I stare at the carton in her hand and wonder if I should tell her it's orange juice. I stand up and walk straight towards the cupboard I know she's looking for and pull out a glass for her. I reach out and hand it to her. Her hand touches mine and she looks up at me and holds it there for a few seconds. My heart starts to race and I quickly pull my hand away.

'I thought you didn't like orange juice?' I say breaking the tension and returning to my seat. I don't want this weird tension between us to go too far again. I don't know if she knows she's doing it, but she's making it really hard for me to keep my distance from her.

'I never said that!' She says looking confused.

'Right,' I say slowly, I'm sure she said that yesterday. 'Tea?' I ask changing the subject.

'Yes, please,' she replies.

I stand up and walk the long way towards the kettle, to avoid getting too close to her again. I feel her eyes following me and when I look up at her, she grins at me. Is she flirting? I try to ignore it and start filling the kettle up with water. When I turn around, Gracie is sat down at the kitchen table, drinking her juice. The juice she told me she didn't like…

'Why are you looking at me like that?' Gracie asks looking amused.

'No reason,' I say trying to forget about it. It shouldn't matter. It's just, has she just lied to me? About orange juice? I try to rationalise, but it doesn't work. It only pushes my brain into a whole different direction. What if she's going crazy or something?

She shrugs her shoulders and finishes her drink, completely oblivious to what's happening right now. I think about asking her, to put my mind at ease when the doorbell interrupts. We both look up towards the door and Gracie stands up. Is she expecting someone?

'I can get it,' I offer casually, standing up and walking towards the kitchen door before she can answer. For some reason, I feel protective, I don't want her to answer it.

'No, I'll get it, this is my house,' she says giving me a funny look. She races out the door before I can reach it. She laughs as I chase her out of the kitchen and screams playfully as I get closer to her. Her giant slippers trip her up and we both laugh.

She gets to the door before me and pulls it open before I can get there.

'Hello trouble,' my smile completely drops off my face. I don't need to see him to recognise that voice. Just the sound makes my blood boil.

'Louie,' I say through gritted teeth. He smiles when he sees me appear behind Gracie. I feel all the heat in my body rise up to my cheeks, along with all the anger I didn't realise I still had.

Why on earth does he feel the need to be here? My anger doubles when I see the look of satisfaction on his face. He's so smug, it's like he knows how his presence is making me feel. I shouldn't be surprised that he's here, this is typical behaviour for Louie. I mean I thought he would've grown up in the last two years. He was always showing up where he wasn't wanted. Louie seems to have a very good talent in causing shit and specialised in trying to ruin my relationship with Gracie at any given chance. He excelled in manipulating Gracie and making me out to be the bad person.

'She doesn't know who you are Louie, she doesn't remember,' I say feeling protective over Gracie and our relationship. I don't even want to give her the chance to speak to him.

'Surely Gracie can speak for herself,' he winks at her. It's not even been ten seconds and he's already manipulating her. I so badly want to punch that smug look right off his face. 'Do you remember me?' He asks, his eyes are glued to her and it's making me feel sick. I hate the way he's speaking to her, even the way he's looking at her.

'No,' she says quietly, so quiet I can barely hear her say it. Louie's smile gets even bigger. It's as if he's amused by this whole thing. How could he be finding this so funny?

'It's been a while, I'd love a catch up,' he says, raising his eyebrows at her. No.

'I, uh,' Gracie hesitates.

'You'd think a person who lost their memory would do everything they could to find out about their old life and I was part of that life,' Louie says looking satisfied.

'Gracie, you don't have to listen to him,' I say finally finding my words and answering for her. I'm desperate for her to tell him no. I know that speaking to him is a bad idea, he is only here to cause problems. It's the only thing Louie is really capable of doing.

They're both silent. It's as if they're telepathically communicating with each other and I suddenly feel like I've gone back two years. I could never understand the hold he had over her. Louie gestures to her to follow him and I watch as she takes a step out of the house. It's like I'm watching this all play out in slow motion and I feel powerless, completely paralysed with no control over what's happening. I panic and reach out to grab her arm but quickly stop myself. I can't just pull her back, that would make me just as bad as him.

'Gracie, if you could just remember, you would know he's bad news,' I shout after her, my final attempt at warning her.

She looks back at me, giving me an apologetic look before shutting the door behind her. I feel sick, that look felt more like pity than an apology. And just like that, she's gone. I'm baffled as to how quickly that happened, just a minute ago we were sat in the kitchen and now she's out there talking to Louie.

Louie. The most manipulative and evil little shit. Gracie has only been home for one night and he's already lurking. How's that fair? It takes everything in me not to follow her out there. I keep telling myself that I'm trying to protect her, that's why I don't want her to speak to him, but I know part of me is scared he's going to mess things up again. Going out there is the worst thing I can do. The more I push, the more she will pull away, that was my mistake last time.

I see Connor's office door open, it's silent in there, he's not on the phone anymore. I peer into the room to see his eyes glued to his laptop screen. He looks completely engrossed in his work, so I decide not to disturb him.

'Who was at the door?' He asks, looking up at me. I guess he did see me standing there.

'Louie,' I say pulling a face.

'Oh,' he says not even trying to hide the disappointment in his voice. It's not just me who hates him. 'Where is Gracie now?'

'Out there speaking to him,' I tell him, trying to hide my anger.

'Oh,' he says again and hesitates, 'I'm sure she is only speaking to him to be polite,' he offers. I know he's trying to make me feel better. I am no stranger to this kind of pity.

'Yea maybe,' I say. It's as if both of us want to stop her but know that we can't. It's her choice if she wants to speak to him, neither of us want to push her. If only she could remember what an arsehole he was. 'What are you doing?' I ask, needing a change in subject.

'I'm about to send an email to one of Gracie's doctors, updating her on Gracie, if she remembers anything and letting her know about some of the short-term memory loss I've noticed too,' he explains.

'Short-term memory loss?' I ask, starting to feel that heavy feeling in my stomach come back.

'Yea, last night I noticed that she had forgotten what we had eaten for dinner.'

'Weird,' I say thinking about the orange juice and if I should mention it.

'I'm just keeping track of it all and letting her doctor know every few days,' Connor explains keeping it light. I can tell he's worried though; we all are.

'Yea, that's a good idea,' I say trying to sound positive. It's scary to think that there could be something wrong with Gracie. I had always thought about her coming back, but I had never considered the impact the last two years would've had on her.

'That reminds me, I need to call Brenda and update her too,' he says after a few seconds. Brenda is Connor's girlfriend. They met last year, a year after Gracie's mum died. I remember my mum being really funny about it, but to be honest it was just nice to see Connor feeling some kind of happiness again.

Andy

'When are you going to tell Gracie about her?' I ask feeling bad that I'm keeping it from her. It's not my news to tell though and I need to respect that.

'When the time is right, I think. I don't just want to throw it in her face,' he explains.

'That makes sense,' I agree. We are both silent for a few seconds, I watch as Connor starts typing on his computer again.

'I'll leave you to it,' I say getting the feeling that I am interrupting and start to walk out.

'Just don't worry about Louie, this time is different,' he says. I know he is just trying to reassure me, but I hope he's right. I know what Louie is like, what he's capable of and how good he is at turning Gracie against me. I nod, grateful for his support and walk out the office. I sit down at the bottom of the stairs and wait.

'What did he want?' I stand up as soon as Gracie walks through the front door, she shuts to door behind her before turning to me.

'Lunch, tomorrow,' she says simply, like it's nothing.

'You're not going to go, are you?' I ask, feeling panicked.

'He didn't leave me much choice,' she says walking back into the kitchen.

I open my mouth to tell her she isn't going before realising I have no right to tell her what to do. I just can't believe how quickly he's managed to worm his way back in.

I stare at her sitting opposite me at the table. I've been trying to reach out to her for days and she's been avoiding me. I finally managed to find her in her kitchen. It took a lot of persuasion to even get her to sit down and speak to me.

'Were you with Louie,' I ask, scared for the answer. The rumours have been circulating around the past few days. I can't stand it anymore; I need the truth from her.

'You're not my boyfriend anymore, it's none of your business, but yes.' She admits it so easily with no remorse or worry for my feelings.

'Gracie, how could you?' I shout feeling my anger get the better of me. 'I don't get it, what happened between us? You can't just decide one day to end it and then just move on with him straight away like nothing's happened between us.'

'Well, I can. I think I've just proved that,' she smirks.

Andy

'Gracie please,' I beg. 'I love you, I know you love me too. I don't know what's going on with you right now but I'm here for you. You should be with me, not him.'

'That's too bad,' she says carelessly, standing up. I stare up at her in shock. She's being so cold, I never thought she would ever treat me this way, it's so unlike her. She shrugs her shoulders and walks off, like nothing has happened.

This isn't her; this is Louie, he's manipulating her. She never acted this way, not until he showed up.

I stare at the open kitchen door feeling my throat tighten. How could this be happening again and so soon? I can already see it. I can't just go in there and pretend that everything is ok. I know that there's nothing I can do to stop her running to Louie, I learnt that the hard way. So, if she wants to, then there is only a matter of time before she does. There is nothing I can do to stop that, the more I hold on the more she'll pull away.

That lump in my throat returns to a familiar place, this feeling isn't new.

I quietly slip on my shoes and walk out the front door. If history is going to repeat itself, then I don't want to be around to witness it.

4

*

Andy: Gracie, if you go with Louie
today, I'm done. I know you don't
remember, but I'm not going through
this with you and him again.

I lie on my bed, staring at the text message I sent to
Gracie's new phone. It's been a few days now and it's still
haunting me. I thought walking out of the situation was the
best thing to do. I thought that it would put things into
perspective for her to decide. If she did decide that she was
going to meet up with Louie, that it was worth losing me
over it, then at least I wouldn't be there to see it.

Well, wasn't that a dumb idea…

I should've stayed, showed her why it wasn't worth it. I am
an idiot. She didn't even reply to me. She looked at my
message and chose not to reply. I sigh and drop my phone
onto the bed. How did I manage to get myself back into
this situation? I didn't want to say it, but I had no other
choice. I can't compete with Louie; he's too conniving and
sneaky.

I know she met up with him, so it's over, it has to be. As
soon as I walked out of her house, I regretted it. I let my
anger get the better of me again and I left her on her own

basically leading her straight into Louie's arms. My brain keeps picturing them together and it's driving me mad. I don't know what it is about Louie, but he has always managed to have a hold over her and I don't know why.

The past few days, I have been waiting to hear something, anything from her. I thought she would at least reply to one of my text messages, but no. She doesn't remember me, or us, in her head she owes me nothing.

I thought going back to work would help me keep my mind off it, but it's just made me more miserable. That's probably why no one invited me out for a pint with them after work tonight. So, I am sat here alone, on a Friday night. There's nothing on TV to distract me, because any normal 20-year-old would be out with their friends. I'm such a loser.

My phone lights up and starts vibrating. I see Connor's name show up on the screen and I quickly grab my phone.

'Connor, what's up?' I try to sound casual, it's a weird time for him to be calling.

'It's me,' I barely hear it, but it's Gracie's voice.

'What do you want Gracie?' I ask bluntly, she has been ignoring all of my attempts to speak to her, so she must want something from me.

'Andy,' her voice breaks, 'can you come and pick me up please?' I immediately sit up when I hear her cry.

'Yes,' I say quickly, without even hesitating, 'where are you?'

'The Rose,' she says. 'I'm going to start walking.' She hangs up and without any more thought, I stand up, pick up my car keys and go.

'I'm just going to give a lift,' I say to my mum as I poke my head through the living room door.

'To who?' She asks, being nosey as always.

'Just a friend,' I say trying to be vague. Gracie and my mum don't exactly see eye to eye. Before she went missing, Gracie and I had a very colourful relationship, not to mention the issues with Louie. My mum doesn't really know what happened, but she saw what it did to me. It seems that even after two years, her problem with Gracie still exists.

'Gracie?' She asks with a judging tone.

'Yes,' I admit not wanting to lie to her.

'This is how she reels you back in,' she explains. 'Then she breaks your heart all over again and you sit there wondering how it happened. It's not good for you.' She begins her speech, the one I have heard too many times before.

'Jesus mum, I'm only picking her up. It's not like I'm marrying her.'

Andy

'Andy!' She warns, 'you know what I mean, I have to pick up the pieces every time, I'm just warning you. It's a cycle, you need to break it.' Easier said than done, I think to myself. I don't want her to be right this time. I know what Gracie is like, but after everything that happened in the last two years, I know what's important. And to me, it's her.

'I don't need a warning, I am a grown up and if I want to go and pick her up, there's not much you can do to stop it,' I say, feeling annoyed at her need to always get involved. It makes me so angry. She is so two faced, telling me that she doesn't like her but being best friends with her dad and pretending that there is nothing wrong. I am sick of it. 'I'm going,' I walk out, opening the front door and slamming it behind me.

I slowly drive down the dark country road, my headlights are lighting up the road. I can't help but wonder what's going on, why she called me and why she isn't with him right now. When I pass the pub, I start to worry that I haven't seen her yet. She probably doesn't remember the way home. After a few more minutes of driving, I see the back of her head and feel relief. I slow down and roll down my window.

'You're walking the wrong way,' I say jokingly, trying to hide the fact that I was actually worried about her. She squints looking into the car and smiles at me. 'Come on, get in,' I say, reaching over and opening the door for her. She climbs into the car and I immediately feel my heart starting to race, even the way she smells sends me through the roof. She looks at me and gives me a shy look. I wait for her to say something, anything that will show me where I stand with her but instead, she turns and stares out of the window.

I sigh and put the car into gear and start to drive. I stare at the road and try not to think about what's going on. I look over to Gracie and she's sat with her head against the window. She looks so sad and it's killing me. I can't take this silence anymore.

'What happened?' I ask.

'Louie was just being a bit of a dick, so I decided to come home,' she explains. The mention of Louie's name sends a rush of anger down my body.

'Why do you have your dad's phone?' I ask.

'I must've picked it up by accident or something, it was in my bag when I was looking for my phone,' she explains. 'Sorry should I have not called?'

'No, I'm glad you called,' I reassure her.

'It's probably good that I had it, you wouldn't have answered it if you saw it was me.' She laughs weakly at her joke.

'Why would you say that?' I ask, annoyed by her comment. She is the one who has been ignoring me, not the other way round. 'I will never not answer your calls.'

'Hardly,' she scoffs. I turn to look at her and she's still staring out the window, clearly trying to avoid a confrontation with me. As much as I want to sit here and call her out on the shit she's put me through these past couple of days, I stop myself. I can tell she's upset and I don't want to add to it.

'So, why was he being a dick?' I ask after a few very quiet seconds. I need to know what this means for her, for me.

'Just being his usual self and I was sick of it, so I left,' she says, keeping her response vague.

'So, are you still with him?' I ask straight up. I need to know where I stand right now and where Louie lands in all of this.

'Andy please,' she snaps. 'Can you just take me home; we can talk about it another time?'

'Ok, yea, that's fine,' I say annoyed that she's not telling me anything, but I can see she's upset; I don't want to push her.

We drive in silence for the rest of the way. It nearly killed me to keep in everything I wanted to say. In the past few days, it has all been building up inside me and when she got in the car, it was hard to keep it all in. I have to wait if I want us to have a proper chance at working.

When we pull up at her house, I promise to call her tomorrow, she nods and gets out the car without saying anything at all. As I drive away, she waves goodbye and just looks so sad. This is all Louie's fault.

When I wake up the next day, the first thing I want to do is call Gracie. It was all I could think about all night, trying to work out what I wanted to say to her. I know I need to approach things differently this time. Louie was able to get in because he was using her memory loss to manipulate her, but now that's over. I can take my time and show her how I feel and how she did before she went missing.

I wait a few hours before trying to call her. I don't want to seem too eager and freak her out.

Then I try to call her a couple more times and nothing.

It takes me half the day to realise that my calls aren't going through to her because she's blocked me...

It's obvious, Louie must have gotten to her again, I just know it. And now she doesn't want to speak to me. I have waited in half the day trying to call her, trying to re connect with her and received nothing back. It's Louie, it has to be. Why else would she not be answering?

This needs to end once and for all. I walk down the stairs, grab my keys from the side, slip my shoes on and walk out of the front door. I hear my mum shouting my name, but I ignore her. She is only going to stop me. I feel numb with anger and stupid that this keeps happening and that Louie

Andy

has managed to get his-slimy-self back into our lives again. Everything was good until he crawled back in again.

'She's made her decision now, so deal with it. No matter how much you stamp your feet like a toddler, it's not going to change a thing.' Louie laughs at me.

'You have no idea what you're talking about,' I say, angry at myself for getting to this point with him. He has no idea what's going on between Gracie and me.

'She's old enough to make a decision for herself, so why don't we just let her decide,' he smirks at me.

'Just stay away,' I warn.

'Well now that you've told me that, I will,' he says sarcastically.

'Louie, I'm serious.'

'Look, mate, I'll stay away, I just can't help it if she comes to me,' he raises his eyebrows.

I bang on the door repeatedly until I hear movement on the other side. Now that I am standing still, I realise that this decision was fuelled with anger and now that I am waiting for the door to open, I realise how much of a bad idea this was.

'Andy,' Louie says, opening the door. He looks happy to see me, what an arse. 'I was wondering when you were going to show your face. To be honest, I thought it would be much sooner than this,' he dramatically looks at his watch. 'Just like old times,' he says rubbing his hands together.

'You left Gracie to walk on her own last night,' I say bluntly trying to think of an excuse as to why I'm here. I knew as soon as he opened the door that it was a mistake coming, but I can't exactly back away now.

'Oh, please, I bet you came and picked her up,' he laughs.

'That's beside the point,' I say awkwardly. His eyes light up.

'Mate, she has you wrapped around her little finger,' he laughs.

'Stay away from her,' I warn.

'I mean, I could, but we all know that she always comes running back to me,' he winks at me. I clench my fists; trying to hold my anger. Louie looks down at my hands and laughs. 'Mate, she really isn't worth it,' he says shaking his head. 'Look what she's doing to you.'

'Shut up!' I warn.

'You want to be careful; she is lying to you and you need to stop falling for her shit!'

47

Andy

'She isn't lying!' I shout. How dare he say that about her!

'Mate, she's faking this whole thing,' he laughs again. How could he stand there and say that about her? After everything that's happened to her, all that she's been through. What a dick!

'No, she's not!' I shout.

'You don't even know the half of it,' he laughs.

I can't listen to him anymore. How could he talk about her like that? He is mocking Gracie, basically laughing at what happened to her and I can't stand to hear it anymore. For me, Gracie coming back with no memory has ruined me, but for him it's all a joke. All these things he is saying, all the lies, I know he is trying to get in between us again and cause even more problems. He failed to pull Gracie away from me so now he's making up lies as a last resort to keep us apart.

I take a breath; I know I should just walk away. What would be the good in staying here and fighting him? Nothing. This is what he wants from me, I know that. I need to walk away. My brain keeps telling me to go but the anger that's inside me is fighting its way out. I step forward, clutching my fists and punch him right in the face. Louie stumbles back, clutching his face and moans in pain.

5

*

I wake up in my bed and the world around me is spinning. My head is pounding and my face aches. My room is dark, but light is seeping through the curtains. What the hell happened? I feel like crap. Just as I start to sit up, my bedroom door opens and more light rushes in. I squint as the brightness penetrates my eyeballs. I lie back down pulling a pillow over my head.

'Andy,' my mum sings walking into the room. She lifts the pillow off my face and I groan. 'How are you feeling?' She asks putting a cup of tea down on my bedside table. Her perkiness is very annoying.

'My head,' I say slowly, feeling the blood pump aggressively around my brain.

'Yes well, perhaps that will teach you to mind your own business and to stay out of Gracie's issues, I told you that you were going to get hurt,' she says, the smugness in her voice radiates off her.

'Thanks for the sympathy,' I reply sarcastically.

'Well time for feeling sorry for yourself is over,' she says opening the curtains. I wince as more light shines in. 'Get up, I called in sick for you, but they want you back on Monday,' she explains calmly, which is her telling me to get my shit together. I look up at her, confused. I thought she'd be more annoyed with me.

'Thanks,' I say cautiously. 'How is Gracie doing?' I ask trying to sound casual but what I really want to know is does she know what happened? Does she care?

'She's fine,' I feel her eyeroll from the other side of the room. 'I've not seen much of her since you shouted at her and blamed everything on her,' she snorts. I almost want to slap her for her smugness. If she wasn't my mum.

'What? When?' I ask.

'Her and Connor came over after we got home from the hospital,' she explains. 'I got you some pretty strong painkillers, so you were pretty out of it, but when Connor and I were in the kitchen, we just heard you shouting at her, so we came in and stopped it. I am not clear on what was said, or what happened there, but the whole thing was probably provoked by Gracie,' she says with a sour look on her face. She can't even hide her hatred for Gracie anymore.

'Oh crap,' I say. I'm an idiot, I've already fucked it with her. 'I need to go over and see her,' I sit up quickly, ignoring the heaviness in my head, I need to fix this **now.**

'Not today, Connor has something important planned for her,' she says before adding, 'I think it might be best to just stay away from her for a while'. I don't want to argue with my mum so I just nod. I will stay away for

Connor's sake, but just for today, she's crazy if she thinks I'm going to stay away for any longer.

For the rest of the day I sit at home, watching TV and trying to distract myself. Things slowly start to come back to me, like drunken memories from a night out. Me, storming over to Louie's house and punching him the face. I cringe at the thought.

I hear a light knocking on the front door and I stand up to answer, slightly worried it's Louie coming for round two. I don't think my face can take anymore; my head is still punishing me for it

'Gracie,' I say softly and very pleasantly surprised when I see her standing on the other side of the door.

'Your face,' she says looking up at me. She looks shocked as she studies it. It takes me a second to realise that she is talking about my black eye. I wonder how it looked when she saw it yesterday.

'It's gotten a lot better, hasn't it?' I say trying to sound positive. For a second, she freezes before nodding and smiling awkwardly at me. I wonder what else happened when I *'supposedly'* blamed everything on her, maybe that's why she's acting so weird with me right now.

'Can I come in?' She asks timidly.

'Yes, of course,' I say quickly, cringing at how eager I must sound. I step aside to let her in. She quickly slips past me and stops in the hallway to take off her shoes.

'Is your mum here?' She whispers.

'She is in the kitchen, but I think she's going out in a bit,' I explain, matching her volume.

'Can we go upstairs then? To talk?' She asks shyly.

I nod and she starts to walk up the stairs. My phone buzzes and I check it to see a message from Connor, he's asking if I'm with Gracie. I let him know she's here and quickly slide my phone back into my pocket. I follow her but keep my distance between us. I don't want to do or say anything that will scare her away now that I finally have her here again. We both walk towards my room in silence. She finds my room easily and comfortably opens my door, walks towards my bed and sits down. I cautiously follow her, sitting down on the other side of the bed. She looks at me expectantly.

'Are you ok?' I ask slowly.

'I'm fine,' she says, fidgeting with her hair. She can't keep still, I think she's nervous, 'it's just been a weird couple of days. My memory keeps blacking out,' she explains.

'I'm sure that's just a symptom of your memory loss, nothing you should be worrying about,' I say trying to reassure her, but I know it's bad. Connor said that it's only getting worse. I can only imagine what it's like for Gracie, it must be terrifying.

'Yes, probably,' she says dismissively. I can tell she doesn't want to talk about it anymore, so I keep in the rest of my support speech. She clearly didn't come here for that, but why is she here?

'Why did you ignore my calls?' I ask desperately, partly trying to change the subject but also, I need to know why. I don't want to admit it, but it hurt.

'I didn't, not on purpose. I didn't get any calls,' she explains. I don't know if I should believe her, but then she's here now. If she wanted to ignore me, why would she come here? I argue with myself trying to work out what I should believe. We sit in silence for a few more seconds, her last words linger in the air. It's awkward, I don't know what to say to her. 'I'm sorry,' she blurts out, 'about everything'. I look up at her in shock. That is the last thing I thought I'd hear her say.

'I'm sorry too,' I reply, the words just fall out of my mouth.

'It's just been so hard, with coming back and stuff,' she explains, 'but I think I have now finally admitted to myself that it's you I want to be with and that I need to stop listening to the little voice in the back of my head saying no. I think maybe I went back to Louie because I was scared,' she admits. Her honesty, if it is honesty, is refreshing. I don't say anything, she is finally speaking to me properly, I don't want to say something that will make her stop.

'So, I'm done hiding from my feelings because I'm scared or whatever is telling me not to,' she says, squinting her eyes shut as if she's scared of my reaction. I honestly thought I'd never hear her say anything like that again. 'So, if you'll have me,' she says quietly. She opens her eyes and looks up at me, waiting for me to say something. She looks so serious; her eyes are glassy and her lips are folded into a nervous straight line. She is looking at me so desperately and I wonder if this is it, this is her coming back to me for good.

'If I'll have you?' I start laughing, mostly with relief. She looks up at me confused by my reaction. 'Gracie, you've always had me,' I say softly, relieving her desperation. 'You're so difficult but I wouldn't have you any other way.' A big smile spreads across her face, making it difficult for me to keep a straight face. I reach out to her and pull her towards me. 'But please, no more trouble, no more drama and no more games,' I warn resting my hand on her cheek. 'I can't take anymore.'

'I promise,' she replies. And then I finally get to kiss her. This time with no more interruptions.

6

*

'You're awake,' I say when I see her sitting up in the bed. I turn my desk chair to face her. I woke up early this morning. I barely slept at all last night. I was so conscious of her being in my bed next to me, I couldn't sleep. I drifted in and out, waking up to make sure she was still there. I ended up waking up really early and after wrestling with sleep for a while, I decided to get up and do something productive white I waited for her to wake up.

Her tired eyes search the room.

'Hi,' she says timidly.

'Are you feeling better?' I ask.

'Yes,' she says slowly, 'I do'. I stand up and walk towards the bed and sit down next to her.

'I'm glad you're feeling better,' I say kissing her bare shoulder. She is sitting there in a vest top and just her knickers. It feels so good to have her back with me. I kiss her collarbone and up her neck.

'I should go,' she says abruptly, pulling away from me and getting out of the bed. I reach out to stop her, but her wrist slips out of my hand. She stands up and picks her jeans up from the floor and starts to slide her legs into them.

Andy

'Gracie,' I say. She ignores me, picking up her hoodie and pulling it over her head. She looks around the floor before spotting her bra and shoving it into her pocket. 'Gracie,' I say again, louder this time trying to get her attention.

'It's ok,' she says opening my bedroom door and rushing out of it. It's ok? What does that even mean?

'Gracie!' I shout standing up and chasing her out of the room. 'Why are you in such a rush?' I follow her down the stairs and see her slipping on her shoes.

'I have a lot to do today,' she says refusing to look at me and opening the front door.

I race her there and place my hand on the door and push it shut. She can't just walk out like that; she looks up at me in shock. It's the first time she has looked me in the eye since she woke up.

'Ok, well maybe I can come and see you later?' I ask, desperate for her not to leave and trying to get any kind of conversation out of her. Why is she suddenly acting like this? It's as if every time she leaves, she comes back like nothing has happened and I don't want to lose all the progress we made yesterday.

'Sure,' she says sounding completely uninterested and I feel my stomach fall to the floor. I lean in and kiss her, pushing her up against the door, hoping it sparks something between us and saves whatever is happening right now. She kisses me back but it's not the same, it's not her. I pull away confused, trying to work out what has changed.

'Gracie,' I say softly.

'What?' She asks irritated.

'Come on Grace, give me a break with all of this hot and cold shit, I can't stand it anymore.' I say desperately trying to get through to her.

'Hmm,' she whispers.

'I know you, stop putting on this front that you don't care.'

'I don't care,' she says simply, like it's nothing, like I'm nothing.

'If you really didn't care, then why did you come here yesterday?' She sighs to herself and for a moment, I think I've got her, that I have revealed her weakness and the reason behind all this crazy behaviour.

'I was bored,' she says slowly, looking straight into my eyes and smirking to herself. Her words sting. I try to ignore that gut wrenching feeling in my stomach, she might as well have just punched me there instead. I look down at her, trying to find the words to protect myself, she has left me completely defenceless. 'Andy, maybe if you stopped making it so easy to walk all over you, then one day you'd be able to find someone just as pathetic as you to love, instead of someone who is way out of reach.'

Andy

'I, uh,' I stutter.

'Take my advice or leave it, it doesn't make much difference to me,' she looks up at me coldly and suddenly I don't recognise her anymore. There's so much I want to say, but no words for it. She uses my shock to her advantage, pulls the door open and slips out the small gap before I can do or say anything else. 'See ya,' she says casually acting like she hasn't just completely ripped me to shreds.

I watch her as she disappears, my brain is trying to make sense of what has just happened. How her waking up in my bed ended up like that. There's no sense to make here. I take a deep breath and try to rationalise, a peaceful second before the pain starts to spread through my body. I feel everything, shame, sadness, anger. She played me, again. And I fell for it, again. She said it herself, admitted it. The worst part, this feeling, the heartbreak mixed with embarrassment, it's familiar. I have felt this before, but that doesn't make it hurt any less.

'Don't you care then?' I ask, grabbing Gracie's hand as she passes me. She turns around and looks at me, there's nothing there, her eyes are dull. The uninterested look on her face says it all. She really was about to walk out of this room without saying anything, after I emptied my feelings out onto her. My last resort in fighting for her.

'Not really,' she shrugs. I stare at the girl in front of me, I don't even recognise her anymore.

'Gracie, please,' I beg. She can't just leave like this, end it like this. She looks more irritated than bothered that I am crying and down on my knees. She hasn't even flinched. How could she just change her mind so quickly, so dramatically, in just **one** day.

She looks down at me on the floor, the way you'd look at a toddler pulling a tantrum in a supermarket. I'm an inconvenience more than anything. My emotion hasn't even touched her, let alone affected her in anyway. She looks up and steps over me, avoiding my touch. Then she just leaves, walks out of the door and just like that, she's gone and it's over. Again.

And just like that, full circle...

Penny

Penny

1

*

I stare down at my phone and look back at my reflection through the blank screen. I've been putting this off, making excuses and finding small tasks that need to be done before I do it. The longer I wait, the worse it will be. I just need to do it. I need to call and tell him that she's back, that his daughter, who we thought was probably dead, is back. I look over to Andy, my son. He is standing there speaking to two police officers, who suddenly appeared when Gracie arrived at the hospital. Finally, the colour in his face has returned. When he saw Gracie, he looked like he had seen a ghost, which I guess, he kind of had. Although, it seems like the shock is finally starting to leave his body. I take a deep breath before clicking on Connor's name and put the phone to my ear. He answers almost immediately.

'Hello,' a muffled, far away voice answers. I open my mouth to reply but the words don't come. This suddenly feels so much harder. 'Hello, Penny?'

'Hi Connor,' I say, finally finding my words.

'Are you ok?' He asks.

'Yes.' I take a breath. 'I have something to tell you,' I say slowly.

'Well, stop being so mysterious and tell me,' he says cheerfully.

Connor and I have been friends since we started school. We were raised together, then we raised our children together. I was pregnant the same time Jennifer was pregnant with Gracie. He was there for me when my husband left me and I was there for him when Gracie went missing and when Jennifer died.

'Are you still there Pen?' He asks. I try to organise the words in my head. I don't know how to tell him, the right way to say it.

'Gracie is back, she's here, I am with her in the hospital now,' I blurt out before I can over think it anymore. I feel bad for just saying it like that with no warning, but I think that's the only way I was going to get the news out.

'What?' He whispers, I contemplate saying it again, did he even hear me properly? I didn't want to tell him this over the phone, but he's on the other side of the world, I was out of options.

'She's safe, they're just running some tests, but she seems ok,' I explain, trying to reassure him and answer the questions I can only assume are going through his brain right now. I hear him down the phone, his heavy breathing, I think he's crying. I try to find the words to comfort my best friend, but nothing feels appropriate right now.

'She's really there?' He asks.

'Yes. She is,' I confirm. 'Now get on a plane and get home.'

'I am, I'm going now,' he says. I can hear the smile in his voice, finally. 'Call me, keep me updated. I can't believe it.'

'See you soon.' I say, hearing chaos down the other end of the phone. Already Connor is doing everything in his power to get here as quick as possible.

I hang up feeling relieved. Telling him was the hardest part and now it's done. I smile, looking up from my phone and see the two police officers walking towards me. One is really tall, with a face like thunder, the other is short, oozing with arrogance.

'Hello Ms Jones, could you answer some of our questions please? Will only take a few minutes,' the shorter officer says looking down at me sat on the chair. I cringe at my name, wishing they would use my maiden name. It's funny how changing your name is so simple, but changing it back seems to be impossible.

'Yes,' I say stopping myself from correcting him and stand up to speak to them.

'It was two years ago when she went missing,' the tall police officer clarifies.

'Yes,' I confirm.

Two years ago, Gracie went missing. The whole thing was very mysterious. Early that morning, Connor and

Jenny received a call from a private number claiming it was the hospital. They were told that their number was listed as an emergency contact and that they needed to come in to identify a body. The woman on the phone ignored their questions and told them they needed to come in immediately. Connor and Jenny left, leaving Gracie asleep in her bed; she was 18, an adult, she would be fine. When they arrived at the hospital, they were told that no one had made the call to them and that there was no one in the hospital who had listed them as their emergency contact. An hour later they got home, went to bed for a few hours and woke up. It got later in the day and Gracie still wasn't awake, Connor went to see if she was ok. He found her bed empty. The police weren't very helpful in the beginning, as Gracie was over 18, they had to wait at least 48 hours. When she didn't come back, the police finally arrived and their whole house was turned into a crime scene. Every inch of the house was checked, nothing was out of place, there was no evidence of forced entry either. Gracie's keys, phone, purse was still in the house, every pair of shoes she owned too. It didn't even look like Gracie had left her bed. It was as if she had just vanished into thin air. There was no evidence or leads, nothing that could help us find out what had happened to her.

It was hard when she went missing. My dislike for Gracie made me feel guilty. We were never really close but a few months before she went missing, it had gotten even worse. I thought she was rude, disrespectful and spoilt. When she started playing with Andy's feelings, I couldn't even stand to look at her. I felt bad that I felt that way about her. I felt guilty that I didn't like her after she was gone. Connor is my best friend, he is family to me, which means regardless of what has happened, so is she.

'Have you spoken to her father?' The short police officer asks, he looks at me with distaste. They didn't like that I insisted on making the call, but after last time, I know how insensitive they can be. I wanted Connor to hear it from a safe place.

'Yes, he is on his way,' I explain.

'Fuck!' I hear Andy shouting; I look around, I can't see him. I hear a loud bang and two nurses rush into Gracie's room, the two police officers turn around and follow the nurses inside. A few seconds later, one of them is pulling Andy out of the room and he's trying to fight them. Everything is happening so quickly; it takes me a second to react to what's happening.

'Andy!' I shout, running over to him and creating space between him and the officers.

'If he doesn't calm down then we will have to arrest him,' the tall police officer warns. I panic, that's the last thing Andy needs right now. I turn around to see him fall onto one of the chairs outside the room. He puts his head in his hands and starts to sob.

'She doesn't remember me!' He says breathing hard.

The Way Back

I sit down next to him and put my hand on his shoulder to comfort him. Even though he's an adult, it still breaks my heart every time I see him upset.

'She's back but she's not here,' he cries.

My stomach drops and I start to feel queasy. Gracie doesn't remember Andy?

I spend the next 20 minutes trying to calm my adult son down and try to convince him that going back in isn't the best idea just yet. Plus, there is no way they are going to let him back in after his behaviour, he's lucky they're still letting him sit outside her room.

Now he is just sitting silently next to me, very tearful. I can imagine after all that stress his head is pounding. I do feel for him, that must have hurt. It's been two years, a very difficult two years for him. I can't recall a day since she disappeared where Andy hasn't mentioned Gracie and then she suddenly comes back with no memory of him. That must hurt. Unfortunately for Andy, he inherits his anger from his dad, which meant he didn't know how to control those feelings and just exploded.

When I finally go into her room, Gracie is standing by the window. She's staring blankly out of it, looking completely lost in thought.

'Gracie,' I say quietly. Her body jerks and she turns to look at me.

'You scared me,' she points out, looking guilty.

'What were you doing?' I ask slowly.

'Nothing,' she replies bluntly. Her attitude seems to be intact; I think to myself. The thought is there before I can stop it.

She watches me as I walk into the room. I quietly sit down on the chair next to the bed, then I watch her slowly make her way back to her bed. She looks at me expectantly, waiting for me to say something. Does she remember me? From the way she just spoke to me, things feel pretty familiar between the two of us. Is what Andy said even true?

'I'm sorry about Andy, he's taking this quite hard,' I explain, hoping her response will give me an answer. Her face is completely emotionless, giving me absolutely nothing.

'That's ok,' she replies.

'Do you know who I am?' I ask straight up.

'No,' the words come out of her mouth easily. She didn't even take a second there to try and remember me.

'Okay, well,' I play along. 'I'm Penny, I'm your dad's friend.'

'My dad? Where is he?' She asks, completely disregarding my introduction.

'He's been working away recently, but he's trying to get back as soon as possible,' I explain. She nods at my response. 'Where have you been Gracie?' I ask, trying to bring the conversation back onto her.

'I don't know,' she replies simply, again no hesitation.

'And you have no memory of your life before you went missing?' I ask wanting clarification, I need her to admit it to me.

'Nope,' she says shaking her head.

I nod. The conversation ends and an awkwardness fills the room. The way she's acting with me, it's as if she remembers that she doesn't like me. I try to rationalise for a second, what would be the point in lying? Unless there is something she's trying to hide, but clearly, she isn't going to give me any answers.

'Right, well I will leave you to be on your own for a while,' I say standing up. 'I'm going to head out and buy you some things that you'll need, I'm sure that will be the last thing on your dad's mind when he gets here.' It's probably one of the only things I can do to help, without having to be around her.

'Ok.' I slowly walk out of the room, my eyes still on her. She is staring back at me in amusement. It's like she's mocking me, she knows I don't believe her but there's nothing I can do about it.

'Thank you,' she says, her voice is suggesting that I'm irritating her.

I give her my fakest smile and walk out.

Andy is still sitting there with his head in his hands. The police officers have left him alone and are now speaking to one of the nurses who was working when they brought Gracie in. I know it's their job to be here, but I feel like they could be a little more sensitive to the situation.

'Is she ok?' He asks desperately. 'Does she remember you?' I look down, feeling sorry for him. Andy always manages to get caught up in Gracie's shit and if she is lying about this then I can already tell Andy is going to get hurt again.

'No,' I say. He sighs quietly, sounding relieved that it's not just him she doesn't remember.

'They said there's no physical damage, so that's good right?' Andy asks desperately looking up at me, looking for some reassurance.

'Yes, it is,' I agree and try to hide my doubt. I know what he's like, it's best for me to keep my theories away from him because it's only going to cause conflict between us. The doctor did confirm before we even saw her that there's no physical damage. The first time memory loss was ever mentioned is when Andy came out of that room. It's possible that it could've been missed by the doctor but it's also possible that Gracie could be lying too. I wouldn't put that sort of behaviour past her either. 'I'm going to run into town,' I say to Andy. 'I don't know what Connor did with her things after she disappeared, so I'm just going to buy her some essentials,' I explain. I'm partly doing this for Connor and partly to get out of this hospital and away from Gracie for a while. 'Would you like to come?' I offer, hoping he will say yes. He needs some fresh air and some time away from this place even more than I do.

'I want to stay here,' Andy says. His answer is disappointing but not surprising. I know it can't be good for him to sit here all day, especially now since he's not allowed in to see her anyway.

'Ok. Just let her be for a while,' I advise him knowing that he hasn't really got much of a choice anyway.

As I walk out, I see one of the doctors who was treating Gracie earlier standing there looking at something on her phone. I stand there for a second awkwardly, wondering if I should interrupt her. She looks up and smiles at me.

'Hello,' she says. 'Are you ok?'

'Hi,' I reply. 'Yea, it's just that Gracie doesn't remember us, she told both Andy and me that she doesn't know who we are.' Her eyes dart immediately down to her notes. This looks like new information to her as well. The surprise on her face is obvious for a second before she composes herself and hides it.

'She has told you that?' She asks, her tone is completely unreadable.

'Yes. So, what does this mean?' I ask. She pauses for a second, like she's choosing her words wisely.

'There are many reasons as to why a person would experience memory loss, but now that we know this, we can look into it more,' she replies. I nod slowly, annoyed by her vagueness. I'm guessing it hasn't even crossed her mind that Gracie is faking it. But why would it? She doesn't know what kind of person Gracie is, most people don't.

'What's that you're drawing?' I ask looking down at Andy's picture on the floor. He looks up, showing off his toothless smile.

'A robot,' he says, admiring his work. I look at the picture, turning my head slightly. It's interesting, I've never seen a robot look like that before.

'Wow, it's very good,' I lie. 'Very cool.'

Gracie looks up from her piece of paper and glances at Andy's drawing.

'It's not. It doesn't even look like a robot.'

I see disappointment appear on Andy's face, he sits up and studies his drawing. I can see him getting upset.

'Gracie means that it's so good that it looks better than a robot,' I say hopefully.

A smile sneaks up on Andy's face and he looks at Gracie expectantly.

'No,' she says softly sounding completely uninterested. 'I meant it looks bad.'

Andy frowns.

'Well, I like your picture,' he says to her and my heart melts.

'Yes, that's because mine is good,' she says simply, looking up at me with a mischievous smile. She looks completely satisfied with herself. It's as if she knows exactly what she's doing, exactly how much her words hurt. I try to remind myself that she's only five…

The next day, I stand at the nurse's desk, staring at my phone and waiting for Connor to get here. He said he wouldn't be long, but I have been waiting for over half an hour now. Gracie has barely looked at me since our first conversation. All night I have been thinking about her, about her memory loss and debating with myself whether she's lying. Faking memory loss after two years of being missing is surely crossing the line? Even for Gracie.

My issue is that Gracie is conniving, she always has been. Even as a child she had this awful mean streak that she hid so easily from everyone else, but I could see straight through it. I'm trying hard not to let our past conflicts cloud my judgment.

Two years ago, it was at its worst, Gracie and I were at each other's throats, it was hard to even be in the same room as her. I didn't like the way she was treating Andy. Their relationship was colourful, but she had him wrapped around her little finger. It was hard to see her treating him that way. I tried to keep my opinions to myself, mostly because it was none of my business. Andy had asked me to stay out of it and also her dad was and still is my best friend. I didn't want to be a grown adult arguing with a teenager, so I reeled it in as much as I could. But the thing is with her, it wasn't teenage bitchiness, Gracie was a full-grown adult bitch and there was a point when I couldn't let her carry on. The last conversation we had, has haunted me for the past two years, my last words to her filled me with regret ever since.

I turn to see Connor rushing down the corridor. He spots me and his face lights up. He looks tired, I'm sure he hasn't slept much since I called. He still looks smart though, but I wouldn't expect anything less from him.

'Finally, you're here,' I say walking towards him.

'I know, finally!' He replies and wraps his arms around me. It feels familiar and good to have him back. Connor to me is family, he's home and has been my whole life. Seeing him now has made me realise why I have been here watching Gracie, making sure she isn't alone. It's all for him. I've been in over my head. I need him right now just as much as he is going to need me.

'How was your flight?' I ask, trying to keep it light.

'Good thanks,' he says quickly, 'where is she? Is she ok?'

'Her room is just through there,' I say pointing to the door.

He nods and takes a step forward. I stop him. He needs to know before he goes in, I can't let him walk in blindsided.

'Wait, Connor,' I say pulling him back.

'What?' He says, his face dropping. He can already tell there's something wrong.

I pause and look around. I asked one of the nurses to be here to speak to him when he got here. I thought it would be easier that way. He might have questions that I don't have the answer to. I smile at her and gesture for her to come over.

'Hi, I am one of the nurses looking after Gracie,' she says walking over to us with a friendly smile.

'Hi,' he says. 'Am I allowed to see her?'

'Yes of course,' she says brightly. 'It's just that Gracie is experiencing some memory loss. She doesn't remember her life before she went missing or much that happened in the last two years either,' she explains. Connor's face drops.

'What? What's wrong with her?' He asks.

'We haven't been able to pinpoint exactly why she's experiencing memory loss, but we're working with her to help that,' she explains.

'Basically, they can't work out why she has lost her memory,' I add.

'Right,' he says, turning around and looking towards the room.

'I'll be five minutes,' Connor shouts as he walks out of the room, leaving Gracie and I alone in the kitchen. I smile awkwardly at her; she ignores me and turns back to staring down at her phone. I'm a full-grown adult, a mother, I shouldn't be thinking this but, eugh bitch!

'I'll be there in a sec Andy,' she says lifting her phone to her ear. She stands up and starts to gather her things off the table.

'You're going to see Andy?' I ask.

'Erm, yea,' she says looking irritated. Andy was so weird with me earlier when I asked him what he was doing today and now I know why. It's because he's meeting her.

The Way Back

'Aren't you seeing that other guy?' I ask trying to sound casual. Andy won't tell me anything. Gracie's eyes light up in amusement.

'And?' She says bluntly.

'Well, if you're seeing someone else, surely you shouldn't be meeting up with Andy?' I ask.

'Jheeze Penny, I didn't think you were such a prude,' she laughs at me. Cheeky bitch.

'Gracie, you know what you're doing. You can't play with people's feeling like that,' I say, trying to be as nice as I can.

'I'm not doing anything wrong,' she says. 'I'm not even seeing Louie.' Liar. I've seen it with my own two eyes and she knows it.

'I've tried to be nice, but it's clear your intentions here aren't good. Stay away from Andy and stop involving him in your little games. You're taking advantage of his kindness and his feelings towards you,' I say sternly. At the end of the day, she's the teenager and I'm the adult. No matter how much she tries to twist this, I will not forget that.

'I'm really struggling to see what this has to do with you Pen,' she says, using the nickname her dad uses for me, as if it's an insult. She's mocking me.

'Andy is my son; it has everything to do with me.'

Penny

'Don't you think you're a little bit too old to be getting involved in teenage drama? You not got anything better to do with your time? I guess that's what divorce does to a person.' Her words wind me, they're cruel, even coming from her. The tension in the room rises and I feel lost for words. I give up with her.

'Everything ok in here?' Connor appears at the kitchen door. I wonder if he heard anything that was said. Gracie looks up at him and smiles. He looks back at her, at his perfect daughter and smiles too. Obviously, he missed her words then, I'm sure it would've wiped that adoration for her right off his face.

'All good, Penny was just telling me about Andy's football game next week. I'm going to go and watch with her.' She smiles sweetly in my direction. I open my mouth to say something, but no words come out.

'Maybe we could all go?' Connor suggests, he looks at me expectantly, waiting for me to say something. For a second, I think about calling her out, right in front of him but then I remember again, I'm the adult and she's the teenager. I can't.

'Yea, that'll be good,' I reply, biting my tongue.

After only a few minutes, Connor walks out the room and sits down on the chair next to me.

'You weren't in there for long,' I point out, looking up from my phone and towards him.

'She needed a minute,' he explains, 'I told her about her mum'.

'What straight away?' I ask.

'Gracie asked where her mum was,' he explains, 'and then she said she wanted to be alone'.

'She needed a minute?' I ask, repeating his words.

'I guess it's a lot of information in one, she needed to process it,' he says.

'Maybe.'

2

*

Connor and I stand there, staring into his house. He was right, it is dark and cold. There is dust everywhere. Even with the lights on, the house just seems so dull. After only two nights in hospital, we brought Gracie home. I really thought she would've had to stay there longer, but the doctors were eager to get her back into normal life. We ended up taking her to my house and she spent the night in the spare room. Connor thought it would be better to take her there. He hadn't been home for months and was worried about what state his house was in. So, this morning, Connor and I woke up early to sort out his house. We left Andy in the house to watch her, although I'm sure Andy wouldn't have it any other way. He has been desperate to spend some time alone with her. He is convinced that it will help to get her memory back.

'I didn't think it would be this bad,' I say looking through the front door, 'it's so eerie'.

'Neither did I,' he admits looking embarrassed. It's bad but he has no reason to be embarrassed. It's been a while since he was last here, no wonder it's like this. 'Let's get this food in the fridge?' He suggests, holding up the bags of food we just bought. I smile and nod, letting him the lead the way.

He walks towards the kitchen and I follow, stopping to open some windows on the way. Something tells me that this house needs more than just fresh air. As I walk into the kitchen Connor is standing by the window opening the blinds. He stares out the window for a second and I can tell his mind has gone somewhere else. I brush off the dust on one of the chairs before sitting down silently; I don't want to interrupt his moment.

'I always wondered why you didn't just sell the house, but now I guess it's good you didn't,' I say. His head lifts up as he breaks out of thought. He comes back to reality and turns towards me.

'I told myself I'd only sell the house when I was sure she wasn't coming back,' he explains.

'So, will you be getting rid of the flat?' I ask.

'I guess so,' he hesitates before answering. I know he hasn't really thought about it, with everything going on it would be the last thing on his mind. But that doesn't surprise me. Ever since Jen died, it's as if he has been walking through life completely lost.

'Will Brenda move in here with you then?' I ask and his face drops. Clearly another thing he hasn't thought of. I wonder if he has even told her that Gracie is back.

'Yea, maybe in a couple of months,' he replies slowly, making me think that this **is** the first time he's thought about it.

We sit in silence for a few more seconds and I can see his thoughts whirring around in his brain. I give him another moment before speaking again. I don't want to let him dwell on things for too long, it's not going to help.

'It's weird being here again,' I say looking around the kitchen and remembering the hours I have spent sitting here. There was a time where I would come over every single day and sit in this kitchen. When Andy's dad left us, we would come over for dinner every night. I couldn't bear to sit at home at the kitchen table we all used to sit at as a family. Jen wouldn't mind, each evening she would welcome Andy and I with open arms and it felt like we were part of their perfect little family. Connor has been my best friend for my whole life, but Jen, she didn't have to show me the kindness she did. As soon as they met, she accepted me as family and for that I am grateful, most woman wouldn't accept the friendship Connor and I have.

I can't help but think about Jen when I'm sitting here. This house isn't the same without her, there was so much warmth, colour but now everything just seems dull. Her death hit us all pretty hard, especially since Gracie hadn't long been missing. Jen was sunshine on her good days, but she also had bad days. It wasn't a big deal, Jen had it under control. I used to be in awe with how she coped with it. She never let it overtake her, that was until Gracie disappeared.

'I know,' Connor agrees, starting to unpack the shopping. He starts spreading the food out on the kitchen counter. He went a bit mad in the shop, I think he just wants to make sure Gracie has enough food, he said he wasn't sure what she liked anymore. I watch as he calmly places each item on the side, he looks at each one carefully and I wonder what is going on inside his head.

'Connor,' I say slowly, feeling my suspicion slowly creep up my throat.

'Yes,' he says looking up, his eyes dart to me and I wonder whether this is the right time to be bringing this up.

'Do you ever wonder about Gracie? About where she's been, have you asked her?' I say timidly. It's too late to go back now, I have already started. I have been waiting for what feels like forever to bring this up and I am not sure when I'll next get him alone.

'She said that she doesn't remember much, just snippets and nothing helpful,' he explains innocently. He doesn't seem to catch on to what I am implying here, he never would. To him, Gracie is his little girl and in his eyes, can do no wrong.

'Do you not question the idea that she was sad about her mum passing?' I ask, taking another approach and choosing my words carefully. I am only bringing this up because I care and I am worried that something else is going on here, I just have a weird feeling. I am not sure how much more hurt my best friend or son can take.

'No, of course she would be sad about her mum dying,' he says brushing it off. He really isn't getting it at all.

'Would you be sad about a person dying if you didn't remember they existed?' I reply bluntly, staring at the wall and avoiding his eye contact. It needs to be said, or at the very least thought about.

'I mean, no, but Gracie has been through a lot and I feel like that information would've been a lot to process,' he says defensively.

'Ok,' I say.

'And you never know,' he adds, 'this could be showing that her memory is there, slowly coming out or something.' He's so naïve, he always has been and that's worrying.

'Connor, have you *maybe* considered that the memory is there?' I say, almost whispering.

'She has no reason to lie,' he says, his voice getting louder.

'Connor, she always used to be up to no good, and she's_'

'Penny!' He shouts hitting his hand on the kitchen counter, I immediately stop talking and look up at him in shock. 'This is fucking hard, I'm in over my head already. I can't have you and Gracie at each other's throats again. Please!'

The Way Back

All the things I wanted to say evaporate out of my mind.

He walks towards the fridge and aggressively pulls it towards him. Reaching behind it, he turns it on at the wall. I watch him, unsure what to say. He opens the fridge and starts to fill it loudly and obnoxiously with food. I feel bad that I've upset him, but I couldn't not say anything. I stand up and walk towards him. He's carelessly throwing his well thought out food into the fridge.

'We should clean it before we put the food in,' I say quietly, breaking the silence. He turns to look at me and I hold my breath cautiously waiting for his response.

'Yea, you're probably right,' he says staring into the fridge. I feel a rush of relief in his response and take it as sign of peace. I know he hates fighting as much as I do, especially now. I walk up to him and wrap my arms around him.

'It's ok, we can get through this,' I say into his chest, repeating the words we have said to each other so many times before.

'Thanks Pen,' he says hugging me back.

I pull away and reach out for the disinfectant spray. 'Let's do this,' I say, spraying him with the bottle. He laughs, grabbing it from me before I can do anymore damage.

3

*

It's been a few days now since my little disagreement with Connor. Since then, I have kept my distance and my theories about Gracie to myself. It's clearly upsetting to him and really there is no point in saying anything else until I have something solid. And anyway, I have planted that seed for him, hopefully it will stick.

This morning has been a busy one. I finally went back to work after having the last week off. It's early afternoon and I'm driving down the high street. I managed to finish early today which is great because I can't stand driving through rush hour. As I drive, I see Gracie walking up her drive. She looks weird, where could she be going at this time? And on her own? I slow down next to her and roll down my window. Her eyes meet mine and she gives me a chilling smile.

I haven't seen her for a little while now. Ever since her and Andy fell out, he hasn't been going over there, so apart from what I have heard from Connor, I don't know much of what's happened recently. All I know is that she has started seeing that Louie boy again. Why can't that girl ever be single? Even after two years of being missing, she has somehow managed to reel in two boys since coming back. Andy is heartbroken again because of her. Although, he told me that he took himself out of the situation, which is progress, because last time it wasn't that easy.

'Well, hello Penny,' she says enthusiastically.

'Where are you off to?' I ask trying to sound concerned.

'The shop,' she says simply. She has a guilty look on her face, like she's up to something.

'I can give you a lift if you want?' I offer.

'No, I'm fine, it's only at the end of the road,' she says.

'Funny you remember that?' I laugh. The bitchy comment leaves my mouth before I can stop it. She looks up at me and a look of amusement washes over her face. I'm challenging her and it looks like she likes it.

'Well, it's not rocket science,' she replies, 'we drive past it all the time.' She folds in her lips, clearly proud of her smart response.

'You look like you're up to something,' I say, not the best comeback ever but I want her to know that I know something is going on. I'm warning her. I know she isn't going to tell me anything; I just want to make her aware that I know there is something going on.

'Ok,' she says slowly. 'Bye Penny,' she dismisses me.

There is nothing more to say so I close my window and drive off. I don't trust what she is doing or where she is going. If she was just going to the shop, then surely she would accept my offer to give her a lift? So instead of driving home, I turn the corner and wait for her to walk past. A few minutes pass when I see her, I wait another few seconds before pulling out onto the side street to follow her. I keep enough distance, so she won't see me. She is walking so slow. I watch as she crosses the road and towards the shop entrance.

She is going to the shop, she wasn't lying. I suddenly feel guilty. This is making me go crazy, I am literally following her. I've gone mad. I sigh, realising I need to get a grip and put my car in reverse just as Gracie stops outside the shop. I freeze. She looks around her before walking past the shop and around the corner.

I slowly drive around the shop to see what she is doing. As I turn the corner, I see her standing in the phone booth with the phone to ear. That is suspicious, maybe I'm right to be worried. I didn't even realise phone booths still worked. Who could she be speaking to? What is so private that she can't even use her own phone? She stands in there for a few minutes, I can't see in because the windows are so dirty. When the doors slide open, I quickly pull away before she can spot me. At least now I know for sure, there is something she is not telling us.

It's been a few hours since I caught Gracie in that phonebooth. It's past 9 o'clock now. I am sitting in the living room watching TV half asleep and debating whether or not I should go to bed. All day I have been thinking about seeing Gracie in that phone booth. I ended up telling Connor that I saw her when he called earlier but he seemed really busy so I decided to keep the rest of the story for when I could see him in person. I keep trying to think of the best way to tell him that something is going on. At least now I have proof and he needs to know.

'I'm just going to give a lift,' Andy says poking his head through the living room door.

'To who?' I ask casually.

'Just a friend,' he says, he's being vague, that can only mean one thing.

'Gracie?' I ask, already knowing the answer. How did she manage to worm herself back in?

'Yes,' he says simply. I can't believe it. From the conversation him and I had the other day, I was under the impression he was done with her. Clearly not. What could've possibly happened in the past few hours for that to have changed? He ought to be warned. Again.

'This is how she reels you back in,' I explain, trying to hide my frustration. 'Then she breaks your heart all over again and you sit there wondering how it happened. It's not good for you.' I can't believe he is falling for her shit again. I didn't think I raised him to be so stupid.

Like I said, Connor is my best friend, therefore Gracie must come with that but that doesn't mean that her and Andy need to have any relationship at all. They are both adults and he is perfectly capable of living his life without her in it. He managed the past two years and if I'm being brutally honest, he was so much better off.

'Jesus mum, I am only picking her up. It's not like I'm marrying her.' His tone goes through me and I have to remind myself that he is in fact 20 years old and there is nothing I can do to stop him from doing what he wants.

'Andy!' I warn. 'You know what I mean, I have to pick up the pieces every time, I'm just warning you. It's a cycle, you need to break it.'

'I don't need a warning, I am a grown up and if I want to go and pick her up, there's not much you can do to stop it. I am going.'

He walks out, opens the front door and slams it behind him.

'Why do you always feel the need to get involved?' Andy shouts. 'This is none of your business but all you do is keep sticking your nose in it.'

'I'm only trying to protect you, to stop you from getting hurt again,' I shout back, shocked that he's speaking like this to me.

'Protect me?' He laughs, 'From what? Eugh she's right. You're jealous, you want me all to yourself, you don't want me to be happy. Just because Dad left you, doesn't mean I have to be miserable too,' he shouts. His words hurt, I would have never expected him to say anything like that. To use my divorce as a weapon. I know they're not his words, they're hers.

'You think I'm jealous? Of what?' I say, feeling bruised. 'Why would I be jealous of a relationship like that? She picks and chooses when she wants to be with you and you just let her?' I laugh.

*'You're only saying this because you don't like her and you literally have no reason to. You're so two faced, being besties with Connor and Jen and then behind their back hating their **teenage** daughter. Grow up!' He shouts.*

'Go upstairs now!' I shout, I can't even look at him. He's so brainwashed by her, there's no way he'd speak to me like that normally.

'No!' He shouts. 'I'm 18 now, you can't tell me what to do, you can't send me to my room. Fuck this, I'm going to Gracie's, where her family aren't complete psychos.' He picks up his phone from the table and walks out the kitchen.

Penny

'Andy, don't you dare leave,' I shout. The front door slams shut, announcing his exit from the house. And I stand there completely alone.

She brings out the worst in him, she always has. I point the remote to the TV and turn it off. If I stay up for any longer, I will just be sat here stewing in anger, I'm better of just going to sleep.

4

*

I stand staring at the boot of my car wondering if I could possibly bring all this shopping in on one trip. Five bags, two hands. I fill up my arms with plastic bag handles, close the boot and stumble to the house. I struggle to get my keys from my mouth to my hands but after a few failed attempts I manage to open the front door. After all that it may have been quicker to make two trips.

As I walk into the house, I drop the bags into the hallway and call out for Andy to see if he is here. His car is sitting outside the house, so I am expecting him to be here. After our little argument yesterday, I am eager to see him. When there is no response, I shrug and attempt to pick up the bags once again. I stumble into the kitchen and jump out of my skin when I see Andy sat at the kitchen table.

'Andy, you scared the living day lights out of me, why didn't you answer when I called you,' I shout. My stomach drops when I see his bloody face.

'Hi mum,' he says sheepishly.

'Hi mum?' I repeat in horror. 'That is all you're going to say,' I shout. 'What happened?'

I rush over to him quickly and take his face in my hands.

'Loule,' he says, a small laugh leaves his mouth. He sounds delirious and his nose looks like its broken. I grab his arm and pull him up.

'In the car, now,' I command.

He is ok. Apparently, it looks worse than it actually is. There is nothing broken and no permanent damage, so now I can be angry. Who does Andy think he is going over there and starting a fight? Although I can't help but blame Gracie. When Andy and I finally got home, I set him up on the sofa and texted Connor to let him know what happened. I told him not to make a fuss, but within minutes he was knocking on my door.

'How is he? Connor asks stepping into the house. Gracie is standing behind him with her arms crossed. I try to hide my disappointment when I see her, but I couldn't exactly say to Connor that I didn't want her to come. She doesn't say anything, she just looks irritated. She's got quite the confidence to be coming over here with a face like that after all she has done today. They both follow me into the living room. Andy is where I left him, on the sofa with a blanket over him and his eyes closed.

'It looks worse than it actually is,' I explain to them, repeating the doctor's words. 'I took him to the hospital and they said that he just needs to rest, that's why I didn't call you straight away. They have given him some medication for the pain,' Andy opens his eyes and looks straight up at Gracie.

'Maybe we should leave these two to talk,' Connor says, taking some invisible hint from Andy. I sigh, not wanting to leave him alone with her, that's how she drags him back in. Reluctantly I follow Connor into the kitchen, I leave the door open and walk over to kettle.

'Tea?' I ask filling the kettle with water and switching it on.

He nods sitting down at the table. I sit down next to him while I wait for the water to boil, neither of us say anything until the kettle starts to come to life.

'So, did you tell her about Brenda?' I ask breaking the silence. Connor had been putting off telling Gracie about his girlfriend for a while now, he was worried about how she would take it.

'I did,' he says vaguely. What kind of answer is that?

'How did she take it?' I encourage him to continue.

'Ok, I guess, she didn't really say much,' he shrugs.

'She couldn't have taken it bad, otherwise then we would know she is lying,' I say. The words leave my mouth before I can stop them, but it's true, Connor just doesn't want to hear it.

Penny

'Penny,' Connor warns.

This is the time to tell him, about seeing her in the phone booth. I need to word it in the right way. I open my mouth to speak when I hear Andy shout. Connor and I look at each other before quickly standing up. Connor strides through the door and into the living room. I follow him. We walk in to see Gracie kneeling in front of the sofa and Andy lying there, shouting in her face.

'We should really let him have his rest,' Connor says interrupting Andy, 'the medication is making him act this way'. He looks towards me and I nod in agreement, although I know full well it was probably something Gracie had said to provoke him.

'I don't know what I said to upset him, I'm so sorry,' she says staring at me with cold eyes. The little smirk on her face shows that she knows exactly what she's doing. That little bitch.

'It's getting late now anyway,' Connor says completely oblivious to what is happening. He puts his arm around Gracie and comforts her. I stand there in shock, watching her react by putting her head on his shoulder. I don't understand how he can't see straight through her. What a brat! I quickly walk them both out of the house before I lose my shit. Connor promises to call and check in tomorrow, I wave them goodbye and close the door. I sigh, I was so close to telling him.

The Way Back

The next morning, I head towards Andy's room with a cup of tea. He can't sleep forever; he needs to wake up. When I walk in, he is awake. He looks terrible but his face looks a lot better than it did, I think blood always makes it look worse than it is. The bruise around his eye looks brutal but the rest of his face looks like it's healing pretty quickly.

'Andy, how are you feeling?' I ask putting the tea down next to him, I try not to cringe at the state of his room. It is definitely not the right time to be bringing it up.

'My head,' he whines.

'Yes well, perhaps that will teach you to mind your own business and to stay out of Gracie's issues, I told you that you were going to get hurt.' I ran out of sympathy yesterday. I hate to say it but if he had just listened to me about getting involved with Gracie again then none of this would've happened.

'Thanks for the sympathy,' he replies sarcastically.

'Well, time for feeling sorry for yourself is over,' I say walking to his windows and rolling up his blinds. I open one to let fresh air in, his room needs it. He is just lying there watching me. 'Get up,' I nag. 'I called in sick for you, but they want you back on Monday,' I tell him, he is twenty years old, I shouldn't have to be doing this for him.

'Thanks,' he says finally making a move to get out of the bed. He picks up his phone and starts scrolling through it. 'How is Gracie doing?' He asks trying to sound casual, I could kill him.

'She's fine,' I say feeling my eyes roll. 'I've not seen much of her since you shouted at her and blamed everything on her,' I scoff. I can't help but laugh. Although, I'm glad he finally stuck up for himself, even if he was drugged up and can't remember it.

'What? When?' He exclaims.

'Her and Connor came over after we got home from the hospital,' I explain. 'I got you some pretty strong painkillers so you were pretty out of it, but when Connor and I were in the kitchen, we just heard you shouting at her, so we came in and stopped it. I am not clear on what was said or what happened, but the whole thing was probably provoked by Gracie.'

'Oh crap,' he says sitting up and finally making a move to get out of the bed. 'I need to go over and see her.' I wish I could shake the stupidity out of him.

'Not today, Connor has something important planned for her,' I explain. Today she is going to meet Brenda. Andy needs to stay out of it. 'I think it might be best to just stay away from her for a while.'

Or forever.

5

*

'You were right,' Andy says, walking into the kitchen. I'm sitting at the kitchen table staring down at an email on my phone. I haven't seen much of him this weekend, he's been very quiet, I didn't even realise he was in the house.

'I know,' I say casually, 'I'm always right.' I look up to see him standing in front of me, my smile fades when I see his face. He looks so sad, like he's been crying. He smiles weakly at my joke and sits down on the chair opposite mine.

'Right about what?' I ask putting my phone down on the table. I already know the answer, but I want to hear it.

'Gracie,' he says sadly. The look on his face is stopping me from saying I told you so.

'Oh.'

'She did exactly what you said she would.'

'I'm sorry I had to be right,' I say simply.

He puts his head in his hands. I'm not sure what to say, it doesn't seem like he wants to tell me what happened, but I'm glad he's finally realised that it's for the best.

Penny

'I've told her to leave me alone now,' he explains, 'I was better without her.'

I nod understandingly. Finally. I try to hide my relief; I don't want to rub it in his face. I just hope he is able to keep his distance this time. I have heard him say he was done with her so many times before, but this time feels different. He doesn't just seem sad; he seems exhausted from it all.

My phone vibrates on the table. I pick it up to see Connor's name pop up on the phone. I click on the message:

```
Connor: Gracie has collapsed, I am on
        my way to the hospital now.
```

'Everything ok?' Andy asks.

'Yep, all good,' I lie, turning the phone face down on the table.

Andy has finally seen through her, hopefully soon,

Connor will too.

Connor

Connor

1

*

I get out of my taxi and walk through the entrance of the hospital, following the blue line on the floor that Penny told me to. I'm trying to keep a casual pace, but I can't help but rush. My nerves are starting to feel out of control, I think I just need to see her. After going up in the lift, turning what felt like endless corners in the corridor, I see Penny standing at the nurse's desk. It's as if she feels my presence as soon as I walk in because she looks up at me instantly and smiles. It's comforting to see her and the fact that she is smiling at me is slightly easing the panic that is rushing through my body.

'Finally, you're here,' she says walking over to me and putting her arms around me.

'I know! Finally!' I reply hugging her back tightly. It has been over a day since I received the phone call from her telling me about Gracie. I was basically alone when I found out, surrounded by strangers who knew nothing about what had happened. I didn't realise how much I needed my best friend's hug until she wrapped her arms around me.

'How was your flight?' She asks pulling away from me.

'Good thanks' I say quickly, eager to get to the point. 'Where is she? Is she ok?' I ask.

'Her room is just through there,' she says pointing to an open door. My nerves peak as I take a step towards it.

'Wait, Connor,' Penny says, placing her hand on my arm and pulling me back gently. The tone of her voice and the look on her face makes me feel uneasy. I can already tell that she's about to tell me something I don't want to hear.

'What?' I say, feeling all my blood rushing to my face.

Penny pauses and looks towards one of the nurses. They have some kind of unspoken communication and I realise that she's been watching us this whole time, clearly waiting for some kind of signal to come over. Somethings wrong. The nurse walks over to us with a reassuring smile, her attempt of trying to make me feel better isn't working. I feel sick.

'Hi, I'm one of the nurses looking after Gracie,' she explains, I try to smile back at her.

'Hi,' I say cautiously, 'am I allowed to see her?' I ask.

'Yes, of course,' she says before pausing for a second; the longest second of my life. 'It's just that Gracie is experiencing some memory loss. She doesn't remember her life before she went missing, or much that happened in the last two years either,' she explains.

'What?' I say, that was the last thing I thought she was going to say. I didn't expect getting her back and her not remember anything. Penny didn't say anything to me about memory loss, I'm not prepared for this. 'What's wrong with her?' I ask, feeling my panic rise. My heart is pounding so loudly, I can feel it my ears.

'We've ran some tests, the good news is that there is no damage that is causing her memory loss, nothing physical,' she explains. I nod, trying to focus on what she's saying.

'So, what does that mean?' I ask starting to feel helpless; I know if Jen were here then she would be asking all the right questions.

'We haven't been able to pinpoint why she's experiencing memory loss, but we're working with her to help that,' she explains, but she sounds positive so that must be a good thing? Ok. I'm trying to rationalise this news in my head. It's bad, but it could be a lot worse.

'Basically, they can't work out why she has lost her memory,' Penny clarifies.

'Right,' I nod slowly. It makes sense but it just doesn't feel real, this whole thing doesn't. I look at them both and try to smile, but it fails. At this point, I just need to see her, see this all with my own eyes. I mutter something that I hope resembles a thank you and turn around.

When I get to her door, I quickly glance into the room and see her lying on the bed. I feel a rush of relief. The whole way back all I could think about was getting here and it not being her. It is her though, it's definitely her.

'Gracie,' I say weakly. As the words leave my mouth, I feel warm tears starting to form in my eyes. She looks up at me and I try to blink them away before she can see them. 'Can I come in?' I ask.

She nods and I walk into the room. Automatically I walk over to her, suddenly forgetting everything the nurse had just said. She flinches as I get too close and then I remember she doesn't know who I am. I quickly and casually try to play it cool and back away, sitting down on a chair near her bed.

'Hi,' she says quietly, she seems nervous too. When I look at her, it feels like no time has passed. At first, I think she still looks the same, but when I really look at her, I notice the pale skin, dark circles and how thin her face looks. She looks weak. It's weird sitting here with her now. I don't feel like myself. I am her dad, but I don't feel like a dad anymore. I haven't felt like a dad in a long time.

'Do you know who I am?' I ask shyly. I need to know if this is true. She stares at me as I speak and doesn't answer straight away. She's silent for so long that I start to question if I said the right thing.

'No,' she finally says. Even though I already knew, I feel shocked by her answer.

'Gracie, I'm your dad,' I explain after a few seconds of figuring out what to say to her. I push away the urge to cry, I don't want to make this harder for either of us.

'Penny told me you were coming,' she explains and I nod, feeling grateful for my best friend. 'So where is my mum?' She asks and my stomach drops. I wasn't ready to answer this question, for some reason I didn't think she'd ask.

'Your mum?' I repeat, giving myself time to answer. I stutter to find the words. I never thought I would be sat here talking to her, let alone having to tell her this. The words are so simple, but it still feels impossible to say. Even after all this time, even after saying it 100 times before, it feels different saying it to her. I feel like I owe her different words, new words, not the ones I've used on other people.

'Gracie, your mum is no longer with us, she died not long after you went missing,' I say finally, forcing the words out of my mouth.

'She's gone?' Her voice breaks slightly.

'She died,' I clarify, regretting it instantly, there was no need for me to. I see the look on her face, she looks hurt. Immediately I start trying to think of all the right things for me to say next. 'I know this might be hard for you, even if you can't remember but—'

'I need a minute,' she interrupts me. Her response surprises me, catching me completely off guard and for a second, I freeze, not knowing what to do or say next.

'Uh, yes,' I say after a few, long seconds my brain finally catches up and tells my body to move. 'Of course,' I stand up and quickly back out of the room.

I close the door and take a breath. It's wrong but I feel relieved that I'm out of the room, but then I feel bad that she didn't want me in there to comfort her. I don't know what I was expecting but it didn't even cross my mind that I'd have to tell her about her mum, let alone so soon.

'You weren't in there for long,' Penny says looking up at me and distracting me from my thoughts. She's sat down on a chair outside the room.

'She needed a minute,' I sit down on the chair next to her. 'I told her about her mum,' I explain. She pulls her glasses off her face and looks at me.

'What straight away?' She asks, I can already tell what she's thinking. I know it would've been better to wait but I couldn't exactly lie to her about it.

'Gracie asked where her mum was, so I told her,' I say simply, trying to justify my actions.

'Then she needed a minute?' Penny questions.

'I guess it's a lot of information in one, she needed to process it,' I explain, trying to understand it myself.

'Maybe,' she says putting her glasses back on and looking back down at her phone. Her reaction annoys me, I thought she would've been more comforting or at least say something that would make me feel better.

2

*

I knew when Gracie got out the hospital, I couldn't bring her back to the house. It was a shit tip and I could only imagine how bad it was because I hadn't actually been there in months. I knew it was going to be cold and dusty, definitely not the place I wanted to take Gracie especially after the two years she had just had. So instead, we stayed at Penny's. Gracie slept in the spare room and I slept on the sofa. Penny was great about the whole thing, welcoming us both with open arms.

Then this morning, I woke Penny up early and dragged her out with me to sort the house out. There is no way I'd be able to do it without her. She made a few comments, but I know really, she wouldn't have it any other way. So, we left Gracie in the house with Andy, I know for sure that he will look after her, probably more than she needs I'm guessing.

'I didn't think it would be this bad,' Penny says as we stand at my front door staring into the house. 'It's so eerie.' It's worse than I thought it would be, it just feels so empty and lifeless.

'Neither did I,' I admit, embarrassed that it's gotten this bad. I can't even remember the last time I was here. The house is so dark and cold. I'm so glad we didn't sleep here last night. Even the thought of spending the night in this house when it's like this sends a shiver down my spine.

'I don't even know where to start,' Penny says sighing. I look at my best friend, feeling slightly annoyed. When I look into the house I feel completely overwhelmed, there's so much to do, the last thing I need right now is Penny's negativity.

'Let's get this food in the fridge?' I suggest, holding up the food we just picked up. We just need to start, otherwise we will never get it finished. She nods in agreement and I walk ahead of her towards the kitchen.

The kitchen isn't as bad as I thought it would be. I walk over to the windows and open the blinds; it looks a lot better with light. I look around the kitchen, everything is where I left it. It feels like the house has been trapped in time.

'I always wondered why you didn't just sell the house, but now I guess it's good you didn't,' Penny says entering the kitchen and sitting down on one of the chairs. That's Penny's way of saying that she was wrong. For the past couple of months Penny has been trying to get me to sell the house, I mean she was right it was eating up all my money, but I knew I couldn't.

'I told myself I'd only sell the house when I was sure she wasn't coming back,' I explain.

'So, will you be getting rid of the flat?' She asks brushing off my morbid comment.

'I guess so,' I say. Although I hadn't really thought about it, but if we're staying here, there's no need to keep it. I bought the flat when I realised that I couldn't sleep in the house, it was an investment I told myself but really it was because I couldn't stand being here on my own. I also couldn't bring myself to get rid of the house, so for the last two years I have been paying for a house that no one was living in, just building up the courage to sell it, or waiting for evidence that would show me I didn't need it anymore. A body.

'Will Brenda be moving in here with you then?' Penny asks.

'Yea, maybe in a couple of months.' I reply. I hadn't even thought about Brenda and how she will be fitting into this. To be honest I completely forgot about her. Trust Penny to remind me about my own girlfriend.

I start unpacking the shopping on the kitchen counter and for a few moments both of us are silent. Me, emptying the bags and Penny sat there doing nothing. This is going to take a lot longer if she isn't going to help. I sigh.

'It's weird being in here again,' Penny says looking around the room.

'I know,' I agree, pulling out a carton of orange juice from the bag. It's weird, it doesn't feel like my house anymore, like my life. I knew things wouldn't go back to normal, it could never be normal without Jen, but I never thought I'd be standing here feeling like a stranger in my own house.

'Connor,' Penny says slowly and I look up at her.

'Yes,' I say matching her tone, dreading whatever she is about to say. I know her too well and she is about to say something that I'm not going to like, I can just tell.

'Do you wonder about Gracie? About where she's been. Have you asked her?' Do I wonder? What a stupid question! Of course I have thought about it, for the past two years it was all I could think about it.

'She said that she doesn't remember much, just snippets and nothing helpful,' I explain nicely, I know now is not the right time to be calling out Penny on her stupid questions, or the fact that she clearly has some kind ulterior motive.

'Do you not question the fact that she was sad about her mum passing?' She asks, this time with caution.

'No, of course she would be sad about her mum dying,' I reply, stating the obvious. She nods in response, looking casually around the room. She's not done, I can feel there is something lurking inside her, wanting to come out.

'Would you be sad about a person dying if you didn't remember they existed?' She asks, the blunt tone in her voice surprises me, it's so emotionless. Her eyes are everywhere apart from on me.

'I mean, no, but Gracie has been through a lot and I feel like that information would've just been a lot to process,' I say defensively. How could she be saying that?

'Ok,' she replies, I don't know what she is trying to say, but I can tell that she is now choosing her words very carefully.

'And you never know,' I add, 'this could be showing that her memory is there, slowly coming out or something'.

'Connor, have you *maybe* considered that the memory is there?' She says quietly, almost so I can't hear it. I look at my best friend, barely recognising her.

'She has no reason to lie,' I say raising my voice and defending my daughter.

'Connor, she always used to be up to no good and she's–'

'Penny!' I shout, interrupting her. 'This is fucking hard, I'm in over my head already. I can't have you and Gracie at each other's throats again, please.' I hit my hand on the counter. I hate when she does this, uses Gracie's past to make a point. I know what she was like but what Penny is accusing her of now is unfair.

'Connor,' Penny says walking into my office. I look up irritated, I came in here to be alone and away from all of it. That lasted all of five minutes.

'Penny, please,' I say feeling a headache lurking.

113

Connor

'Connor,' she says again, sitting down on the armchair in the corner of the room. I consider asking her to leave me alone, it wouldn't be the first time and I know it definitely won't be the last either.

'What is it Penny?' I say, letting my irritation show.

'You know what she's like, she was antagonising me on purpose. She knew exactly what she was doing, exactly what she was saying,' Penny complains. I look down at my desk and wonder how hard I would have to bang my head on it to knock me out. Hypothetically of course.

I think back to 10 minutes before, where we were all sitting having a nice dinner together. Jen, Penny, Gracie, Andy and me. It was all going ok, I guess. I mean, it's been a while since we've all been able to sit at the dinner table and have a civil conversation, but I thought since Gracie and Andy were on good terms at the moment, things would be ok.

I was wrong. Of course, the topic of divorce came up in conversation, where Gracie very candidly shared her views on it. And of course, those views were conveniently the opposite of Penny's views. It seems that the touchy subject for Penny was an amusing one for Gracie. The rest of us knew what was good for us and proceeded to keep quiet for the duration of the conversation, Gracie however, seemed to know exactly which buttons to press with Penny.

'I do know what she's like,' I admit, knowing full well the extent of my teenager daughter's bitchiness.

'Are you going to say something to her?' She asks, her question feels more like a demand.

'Penny, I can't tell her off for sharing an opinion,' I say, instantly regretting my choice of words but I know for a fact if I were to say something, Jen would not be happy with me. Although Gracie's response to Penny was very controversial, she's entitled to her own opinion.

'Connor, what the hell?' She exclaims. I look at her in amusement. I've not heard that phrase come out of her mouth since we were in at least our twenties. Watching her in front of me now, getting upset about this takes me back to when we were teenagers, where I'd spend hours listening to her bitch about Jessica Finley.

'Oh my god! Pen! Listen to yourself,' I say.

'Connor! She started it!'

'Yes, she did. But she's a teenager and you're an adult!' I exclaim, pointing out the obvious. I almost want to laugh about how pathetic all of this is. Which is better than before, when I couldn't stand to even sit there and listen to it.

'I know but Connor.'

'Penny, I came in here to get away from it, not for you to follow me in here. Please, leave me alone,' I say, finally having enough of it. 'Like I said before, I'm not

115

getting Involved with this anymore. As much as you are my best friend, she's my daughter. I really don't get what you want me to do here.'

She gives me one of her death stares, which doesn't bother me. I've survived enough of them in my lifetime. I know she'll leave but like always, things will blow over in a few days.

I pull out the fridge and reach behind it to turn it on at the wall. How could she be sitting there saying that? How dare she? I push the fridge back, making Penny jump as it hits the wall. As my best friend she should be making me feel better, not worse. Why does she always do this? Why can't she put aside her feelings towards my daughter for now, for me.

Penny watches as I open the fridge and start filling it. I'm throwing things in carelessly, taking my anger out on the innocent food. Penny walks up behind me and taps me lightly on the shoulder.

'We should clean it before we put the food in,' she says quietly. I look at the fridge, the smudged shelves, with food crumbs and God knows what else. I hate that she's right.

'Yea, you're probably right,' I say turning towards her but staring at the wall behind her. I still can't look at her. She takes a step in front of me and looks up at me. My eyes flicker for a second onto her and our eye contact

116

breaks the tension. She takes a step forward and wraps her arms around me and I let her.

'It's ok, we can get through this,' she says into my chest.

'Thanks Pen,' I say hugging her back. My anger slowly evaporates. She pulls away and looks up at me. For a second, I think she's going to say something else, but instead she reaches out for the disinfectant spray on the kitchen counter.

'Let's do this,' she says, spraying me.

Connor

3

*

We were finally able to get the house finished and Gracie settled in. We had a quiet evening and spent some time together. I was going to tell her about Brenda, but I just couldn't bring myself to do it yet. It just seems too soon. Especially since in her mind, her mum only died two days ago. Not that she remembers her mum, but still.

I had to wake up early this morning for a meeting. They are still making me work but they are letting me do it from home. I guess there is no official time off given when your missing daughter of two years comes back. I have been on the phone for the past hour talking about things that just don't seem important anymore.

I finally get off the phone and end the meeting. I was sick of listening to my colleague talk for so long, about what felt like nothing. I pull my laptop out of its bag and place it on my desk. The screen lights up and suddenly turns off again. The battery is dead. I very quickly become irritated, I charged it so this wouldn't happen and now it's dead. I feel my frustration rise and realise that I need to get a grip, why am I getting angry about my laptop dying? I open my bottom draw to retrieve the charger and clumsily plug it in. The front door slams and grabs my attention immediately. It was so loud and now I can feel my heart pounding. Who was that? Before I can panic even more, Andy appears in my doorway.

'Who was at the door?' I ask trying to pretend that I didn't just have a mini heart attack.

'Louie,' Andy says rolling his eyes, the feeling is contagious.

'Oh,' I say not bothering to hide my disappointment. I hate Louie. 'Where is Gracie now?'

'Out there speaking to him,' Andy moans, I fight the urge to stand up and stop her. The last thing Gracie needs right now is Louie making things complicated for her. All that boy knows how to do is to cause trouble.

'Oh,' I say again feeling helpless. I can see in Andy's face that he's feeling insecure and I don't blame him for that. 'I'm sure she is only speaking to him to be polite,' I offer. I don't like the fact she is out there speaking to him either, but there isn't much I can do about that. How can I try to parent her, especially after her being on her own for the past two years?

'Yea, maybe,' he replies staring down at his feet. I open my mouth to say something to reassure him and then stop. I don't want to upset Gracie again by getting involved, she was right the last time, it really isn't any of my business. 'What are you doing?' Andy asks changing the subject. Thank God.

'I'm about to send an email to one of Gracie's doctors,' I say, moving the mouse on my laptop to bring it back from the dead. 'I'm just updating her on Gracie's memory loss, if she remembers anything and letting her

119

know about some of the short-term memory loss I've noticed too,' I explain.

'Short-term memory loss?' Andy asks.

'Yea, last night I noticed that she forgot what we had eaten for dinner.' It was very strange, she just got confused all of a sudden when we were discussing what kind of food she liked to eat now.

'Weird,' Andy says.

'I'm just keeping track of it all and letting her doctor know every few days,' I explain downplaying it. I don't want to worry Andy any more than he already is. I feel so bad for him, I can see that this is killing him. I couldn't imagine how he is taking her memory loss and how he must be feeling now that Louie has shown his face.

'Yea, that's a good idea,' Andy says.

'That reminds me, I need to call Brenda and update her too,' I tell him. I keep meaning to do that and forgetting. I'm still getting used to a life with both Gracie and Brenda in it.

'When are you going to tell Gracie about her?' He asks, I know he doesn't like the idea of knowing and not being able to tell Gracie, but I want to give her some normality before I bring the new in.

'When the time is right, I think, I don't just want to throw it in her face,' I explain.

'That makes sense,' Andy says. His agreement is comforting, I was worried he would tell her before I could. I nod in response when I'm suddenly distracted by an email popping up on my screen. My eyes dart to it.

'I'll leave you to it,' Andy says getting my unintentional hint and backing out of the room.

'Just don't worry about Louie, this time is different,' I lie trying to reassure him but who knows what's going to happen this time round...

4

*

'I got us some milk,' I say holding up the carton as I walk into the kitchen. Gracie is standing at the sink, facing the window. She turns around and smiles at me.

'Gracie already got some,' I turn to see a smug Louie sitting at the kitchen table. I frown before I can control my face. I was wrong the other day; turns out that this time isn't different. Louie somehow managed to worm his way back in with Gracie and I haven't seen Andy since. Every night this week, I've come home from work and Louie's been here. But what can I do about it? How could I possibly parent her after failing so badly the first time?

'No, I didn't,' Gracie says looking confused.

'Yes, you did,' Louie says slowly. I hate the way he speaks to her, like she's stupid.

I ignore him and walk over to the fridge. The tension rises as I realise that they're both watching me, waiting to see who's right. I open the fridge door and my eyes immediately dart over to a full carton of milk in the side of the door. For fuck sake, Louie was right. I look over at Gracie and I can see that she's looking at me and waiting for confirmation.

'Seems like you did,' I say cautiously. Gracie frowns as confusion washes over her face. I can see from the look on her face that she can't remember getting it. It seems that whatever this is, it's only getting worse. 'Don't worry Gracie, you're suffering from memory loss, things like this are bound to happen,' I say trying to reassure her, but I'm lying, this isn't normal.

I can see that Gracie is lost in her own head now, trying to work out what's happening and I hate seeing her like that. I can't imagine what it's like for her. Louie stands up, interrupting the silence by sighing loudly. He brushes the whole thing off like it's nothing and stretches his arms up to the ceiling. His fingertips brush the ceiling and it makes me think back to what my mum used to say about not touching the walls.

'Anyway, ya freak, I'm off, I'll see you later,' he says with a huge smile spreading across his face. He looks amused. What part of this is amusing? He looks at me and nods goodbye, I ignore him of course but that doesn't seem to bother him. I really don't see what Gracie sees in him; in fact the whole thing is really bizarre to me, it always has been.

I open the front door and walk into the house, Louie and Gracie are standing there, staring at me. They both look furious, I have definitely interrupted something here. I cringe, knowing it's too late to hide any of this from Andy; he's right behind me.

'What's going on here?' I ask cautiously, walking into the house. I feel bad that there's nothing I can do to warn Andy.

'Nothing,' Gracie says. 'Louie, you should go,' her voice is quiet. I know that I've definitely interrupted something here. She looks sad and I can quite easily bet on who's made her feel that way.

'Yes, you should,' Andy says, appearing in the door behind me. I feel myself stepping in front of Andy, protecting him. I don't want a repeat of last time between the two of them. The tension rises and I can feel myself getting angry that Louie is here. Louie completely ignores us and looks towards Gracie, as if he's waiting for her to say something else, to ask him to stay or something.

'Fine,' he says after a few long seconds. I feel relieved, I didn't want her to want him to stay. He storms past us and out of the door. Gracie refuses to look at either of us.

'What was all that about?' Andy asks her.

'Nothing, it was nothing.' Gracie says looking completely unbothered now, any emotion that she was showing a few seconds ago seems to have left with Louie. 'Nothing that concerns you anyway,' her harsh words hurt Andy, I can tell by the look on his face. I feel bad for him, I have felt bad for him through this whole thing.

'Please, Gracie just talk to me,' Andy begs, his voice sounds so broken.

Gracie ignores his pleas and starts walking up the stairs, leaving Andy and me alone. When I look at him, I feel awful that she's treating him this way. I feel responsible. I follow Gracie up the stairs, taking two at a time to catch up with her. When I finally reach her, she's already in her room sitting at her desk.

'Gracie,' I say softly. 'At least talk to him.'

'Why? Because my dad said so?' She says sounding pissed off.

'No, because look at him, look at what all of this has done to him,' I say, trying to find the right words for her to understand.

'He's 18, he's an adult,' she says bluntly. 'He can handle it.'

'Gracie, come on,' I warn, starting to get angry at her.

'What about me, Dad?' She says raising her voice, it takes me by surprise. I've never heard her shout at someone before, let alone at me. 'How about how I feel? About my happiness?' Her question throws me, I didn't expect her to say anything like this.

'All I'm saying is Andy is–'

'Andy is what?' She asks. 'Sad, upset, heartbroken? And! Does that mean because Andy's feelings are hurt, I have to go back and be with him?

Because he's your precious little best friend and you'll do anything to make him happy.'

'You know that I –'

'No,' she says, interrupting me again. 'I'm your daughter, you shouldn't be taking my ex-boyfriend's side, no matter how close you are with him. All I've done is move on, I haven't done anything wrong. You can't tell me who I can love!' She shouts.

'But you keep going backwards and forwards, you can't see what it's doing to him!' I shout back, finally getting my words in.

'And, regardless of what's happening. It's none of your business, am I breaking the law, no? You can't punish me for this!'

She's right, I can't tell her off and from a parent's point of view, she isn't doing anything wrong. I want to tell her off, but that's not my place as Andy's friend.

'Gracie,' I say quietly.

'We are never going to agree on this, but we really don't have to, this is my life. You need to stay out of it, otherwise, you will end up having to pick a side at some point. And something tells me it won't be mine,' she says as a matter of fact.

'Ok,' I say simply, there's nothing more I can say.

'So, what's for dinner?' Gracie says, slipping onto the kitchen counter. Her mood has lightened but I can tell what just happened is still weighing down on her.

'I was thinking pasta,' I say. I know we don't have anything else; I really need to start getting better at this dad thing. I have never really been responsible for this kind of thing before and it's obvious I am failing at it. It doesn't seem that Gracie has noticed though, so that's a positive.

'Great,' she says as she watches me fill the kettle and turn it on.

'Have you spoken to Andy at all? He's been asking after you,' I say trying to sound like I'm casually starting a conversation with her although that really isn't the case, I'm being nosey.

'I haven't heard from him at all,' she says. I wince. That's not true. Andy told me earlier that he's been trying to get hold of her and she's been ignoring all of his calls and texts, she is lying to me. I feel my stomach sink and my mind goes straight to Penny. Since Gracie came back Penny has been making comments and for the first time I'm considering if there is any truth to them. And then I feel guilty. After everything Gracie has been through, I shouldn't be accusing her of lying. It's nothing I try to tell myself, just a small red flag. My last conversation with Penny lingers in my brain, it was a few hours ago, she called me while I was working.

'I was actually talking to Penny earlier, she said she saw you,' I say.

'Oh really? Where?' She asks.

'She saw you walking down the street,' I say slowly, looking for a reaction.

Of course, Penny called me as soon as she saw Gracie. She said that she saw Gracie and that she was acting weird. I didn't get the full story, I told her I was busy and couldn't talk, I was tired of hearing it from her.

'That's odd,' she says. 'It must've been someone else, I haven't left the house today.' Another lie passes through her mouth like it's nothing.

'She said you spoke,' I add testing her. She looks at me as if I'm crazy, but she must've left the house today to buy the milk. That means what Penny is saying is the truth and if Penny is telling the truth, then Gracie is lying. Or it is the truth for her because she can't remember.

'Weird,' she says brushing it off, adding no other explanation. She's completely unfazed, unaffected by this conversation. I can't tell anymore but what would be the point in lying? 'Anyway, I need to get ready for later, call me down when it's ready.' She slips off the kitchen counter. As she walks away, I realise that I never got to say what I came back from work to tell her.

'Wait!' I call after her. 'I want to speak to you about something.'

She turns around and walks back to me. I realise then after the conversation we just had that perhaps this isn't the right time to be bringing this up, but then like I said she seems completely unfazed by it. She looks at me expectantly and waits for me to speak. No time like the present.

'So, there's something I have been meaning to tell you, I've not kept it from you, I just wanted to wait until the right time,' I explain repeating the words I had been rehearsing on the way back from work. She nods and I think for a second before blurting it out. 'I have a girlfriend.' Her smile falls and her eyes widen. Only for a split second before her face relaxes. It was barely noticeable.

'Since when?' She asks bluntly.

'For a few months now,' I explain.

'Right,' she says slowly. Her eyes are glued to the floor. I don't know what to say now, her response has made it difficult to reply.

'You will meet her soon,' I add hoping that will spark more of a conversation, let her ask any of the questions she wants to.

'Ok,' she says, her eyes are still refusing to look at me. What even is this reaction? She isn't giving anything away. I open my mouth to say something else when she looks up at me. 'Can I go now?'

'Uh,' before I can answer, she walks out of the kitchen.

I honestly can't tell if that went well or not. What even was that? I listen to her footsteps as she walks up the stairs. When I hear her bedroom door shut, I pick up my phone and start adding to my notes on my phone about the milk, I can't forget to mention this to the doctor.

5

*

The next evening, I park my car outside the house, turning off the engine and lights. I reach over to the passenger seat and grab the white plastic bag with Gracie's and my food in. I decided that ordering food in tonight would be a better idea since last night's pasta was a disaster. I am secretly hoping the good food will encourage Gracie to speak to me more about Brenda. Yesterday she ate her dinner so quickly I wasn't even able to sit down and eat with her. I keep telling myself it was because she was going out and was rushing to be ready rather than the other reality of her just wanting to avoid sitting down and speaking to me.

I sigh and get out the car. This bag is much heavier than I thought it would be, we definitely ordered too much food but at least I know Gracie's appetite is healthy. I reach in my coat pocket for my keys and start fiddling through everything attached to my keyring to find the key for the front door. I unlock and open the door to see Louie and Gracie standing there staring at each other. I feel *deja vu* when they both turn to look at me. The tension is high. I have definitely interrupted something. Again. Louie looks furious.

'Are you going to tell him, or am I?' Louie asks and I get that gut sinking feeling. He looks to Gracie and her eyes are wide, as if they're warning him.

'Tell me what?' I ask putting our food down on the floor. I stare at them and wait for one of them to say something. Both of them stay silent and I feel myself becoming impatient.

'Gracie has been lying to you this whole time,' he starts. The fear that's been lurking inside me this whole time about Gracie starts to grow. I look at Gracie and she is shooting daggers at Louie. The tension between them is high. I feel my pulse racing. He needs to say something before I have a full-on heart attack.

'There is two of them. She has a secret twin.' He blurts out and I feel a rush of relief. Gracie's face softens into a smile. I really thought he was going to say something else, something worse.

'Twins!' I repeat, starting to laugh. 'Good one.'

Twins, not possible, nowhere near possible. Louie is standing there; his breath is heavy and his cheeks are flushed. He has gotten himself all worked up and I feel sorry for him. Perhaps whatever bullshit he was putting on Gracie stopped working and he somehow thought pulling something like this would work?

'Right, well done, you got me,' Gracie says sarcastically and I laugh. We both look at him like he's mad, well he must be if he's shouting that Gracie has a secret twin! Like where has that come from?

'Maybe you should go,' I suggest opening the door, 'it's our dinner time and there's not enough food for you.' I look at Louie, shaking my head at him and tighten my lips into an awkward firm line. The silence makes **me** feel no longer welcome in the conversation, so I walk into the kitchen and leave the two of them alone.

'What was that about?' I ask when Gracie finally walks into the kitchen. I've been waiting for at least 10 minutes.

'I honestly have no idea, he just snapped when I told him it was over,' she explains. I want to believe her but how could someone get so upset and say such crazy things over that. I fight the urge to ask her more about it, it's none of my business and the fact that she's chucked him should be good enough for me.

I start emptying our food onto the kitchen table. My mind is full of thoughts that I am trying to push to the back of my brain. I walk over to the cupboard and get us a plate each, Gracie watches me as I pass her a plate. She looks up and smiles weakly at me. *What is going on with you?* I want to scream at her. She looks away and focuses her attention on opening the food containers. I reach out to help her when my phone starts to vibrate. I pick it up and stare at the screen.

'Oh crap!' I say looking at a message from Penny.

'What is it?' Gracie asks.

'Andy went over to Louie's earlier, started an argument with him,' he explains.

'And,' Gracie says, starting to fill her plate with food.

'Well, Louie didn't like that and now Andy's pretty hurt,' I explain. 'Did Louie say anything to you when he was here?'

'No,' she says, 'he wasn't here for that long'.

'I told Penny we'd be over there right away,' I say walking to the back door and sliding on some shoes. I lock the door, pick up my phone and keys and put them in my pocket. I look over to Gracie who is just sitting there, pouring even more food onto her plate carelessly. Does she not care? I stare at her in disbelief.

'Let's go,' I say abruptly, she looks up at me and for a second just stares at me before rolling her eyes and standing up. She slowly walks out of the kitchen and sits down on the stairs. I watch as she slowly puts on her trainers, taking time to ensure each shoe is tied correctly. I feel my blood beginning to boil as she puts her coat on.

Come on, I want to shout but I stop myself. She couldn't have taken any longer then, her attitude surprises me. I know her and Andy aren't really on speaking terms at the moment, but I would've thought she'd have still cared. I walk out the door and towards Penny's house, leaving Gracie to walk behind me, I can't stand to look at her right now.

The Way Back

When we arrive at Penny's, she answers the door within seconds, greeting us with a dull smile, she looks completely wiped out. She politely invites us in and both Gracie and I walk through into the living room. The house is lifeless, so quiet and the living room is dark with only a lamp and the light from the TV giving it life. Andy is lying on the sofa with his eyes closed. The dim lighting reveals a black eye starting to form on his face. His nose is swollen, almost doubling in size, it looks like he took a right beating.

'How is he?' I ask.

'It looks worse than it actually is,' Penny explains. 'I took him to the hospital and they said that he just needs to rest. That's why I didn't call you straight away.' I get that, but I just wish she told me earlier, I could've gone to the hospital with her. Although, it's probably better that she didn't say anything, otherwise Louie wouldn't have made it out of the house so easily earlier on. 'They have given him some medication for the pain.' I look down at him, at his face and how messed up it looks. How could this happen again? What was he doing going over there? What did he think was going to happen? Andy's face squirms before his eyes open and shoot straight over to Gracie, taking no notice of anyone else in the room.

'Maybe we should leave these two to talk,' I suggest nudging Gracie playfully and trying to break the bad mood she seems to be in. I can feel Penny's reluctance but after a few seconds she follows me into the kitchen. I sit down at the kitchen table and she puts on the kettle.

'Tea?' She asks and I nod in response. She walks towards the table and sits opposite me while the kettle starts to boil. 'So, did you tell her about Brenda?' She asks, getting straight to the point then I guess.

'Yes,' I reply simply, not wanting to give away too much information.

'How did she take it?' She's fishing for information and I consider lying to her. I know it would probably make things easier. Penny will be looking for any kind of cracks in Gracie's story, but I know; at least I hope, it's coming from a good place.

'Ok, I guess, she didn't really say much,' I explain.

'She couldn't have taken it bad, otherwise then we would know she is lying,' she says and I immediately regret even giving her a little bit of the truth.

'Penny,' I say bluntly, warning her. She looks up at me as if she's shocked that I raised my voice. That look annoys me, I don't know what she was expecting me to say to that. I am sick of this constant accusation of Gracie's story. We can't even have one conversation without her bringing it up.

Before I can say anymore, Andy's voice erupts in the living room. Penny and I both look up in surprise and I stand up and rush into the living room. When I walk in, I see Andy lying there, blindly shouting at Gracie and she's just sat there, taking it. What the hell is going on? How could anything escalate this quick? Before Andy says something he regrets or Gracie can get any more upset, I intervene.

'We should really let him have his rest,' I say standing between them. Gracie stands up and takes a step back, 'the medication is making him act this way.' I turn to her and explain the only reason as to why Andy would be shouting like this.

'I don't know what I said to him to upset him, I'm so sorry,' Gracie says looking panicked. She looks genuinely upset by this and I feel awful for her. I put my arm around her to try and comfort her, for the first time she doesn't flinch.

'It's getting late now anyway,' I say looking to Penny, I need to get Gracie out of here. The stern expression on her face breaks and she nods in agreement with me. With no more words, Gracie, Penny and I walk towards the front door. The awkwardness is uncomfortable and when Gracie steps out the house I turn to Penny and promise to call and check in tomorrow. There's so much tension and I have no idea where it has come from, whatever is going on between Gracie and Andy, it seems to have affected Penny too. I step out of the house and pick up my pace to catch up with Gracie. I try to think about what I should say to her, what I should say to make her feel better about this.

Connor

'I can't wait to eat, I am so hungry,' she says turning to me with a huge smile spread across her face. I stare at her in shock, seconds ago she was almost in tears and now, she's completely fine…

6

*

'Surprise!' I jump out of my seat in shock as I hear the voice echo through the house. I look down at my newly made, hardly drank cup of tea spilt onto the living room carpet. The hot, milky water is already absorbed into the cream carpet. Crap. I look up and see blonde appear at the door. My eyes focus and straight away catch her blue eyes. The first thing I always notice on her, the first thing I noticed when I met her. Brenda.

'Wow, Brenda.' I say trying to hide the look of horror on my face. I really wasn't expecting her today. Gracie is upstairs and I haven't prepared her for any of this. Brenda's smile sinks and I can tell I didn't hide it quite as well as I had hoped.

'Shall I come back another day?' She asks playfully and I feel the tension ease.

'No, not at all,' I say. 'You just surprised me,' I open my arms gesturing for her to come forward. She awkwardly hugs me; I haven't exactly made her feel welcome. She places her bags on the floor and sits down on the sofa opposite me.

'How have you been?' She asks reaching down and picking up my split drink and carefully placing it on a coaster. I watch her as she studies the stain on my floor, I can tell she's already thinking about how to clean it up. I smile at her sweetness and realise just how long it's been since I've seen her. Even before Gracie came back, I was working and travelling a lot.

'Well, things are getting better since I last spoke to you,' I explain. I have really been trying to keep her updated and in the loop. I never wanted her to feel left out, but in the last few days it has been a bit difficult. Perhaps that's why she's here. As I explain she nods, listening carefully to me. I tell her about the last few days, including all the drama with Andy. It feels good to tell her, I know that she's listening and not once does she interrupt me or question any of Gracie's intentions.

'So, when can I meet this lovely Gracie?' She asks when I finish.

'Oh yes,' I reply suddenly remembering she's upstairs. 'Gracie. You must meet Gracie.'

Before I can overthink how this interaction is going to go, at the top of my voice I shout for her to come down. Brenda seems startled by my voice and I smile at her in apology before shouting again when I don't hear any response from Gracie. This time Brenda looks at me with concern and I wonder what I must look like. I'm nervous and I can feel it pushing through my body like adrenalin, I'm running around like a mad man.

'I'll make some tea,' I suggest, knowing that I can't just sit here and wait. Besides, I might as well do something productive. I jog into the kitchen and then realise that the last of the milk is now absorbed into my carpet. I turn back on my heel and walk back into the living room and sit down. Brenda looks at me confused, 'we don't have any milk.' I explain.

She gives me a worried look, but I ignore it. I know what she must be thinking, I know I'm acting weird, but I can't help it. I'm nervous and my body is struggling to cope with the feeling. Gracie pokes her head through the living room door and I stand up again. She looks at me expectantly before her eyes cross the room towards Brenda. Her face drops.

'Gracie, this is Brenda.' I try to say confidently, but my voice gives me away. Both Brenda and I stare at her, waiting for her to say something but she just stands there in silence.

'Tea?' Brenda asks, I know she's trying to break the awkwardness.

'We don't have any milk,' I say again, feeling irritated having to repeat myself.

'Why don't you run out and get some?' She suggests giving me an encouraging smile. 'Gracie and I can get to know each other while you're gone.' Her comment throws me, I don't want to leave them alone, but I can't really say that to her. It's not that I don't trust her, I just want this to go well and I can already tell Gracie is in one of her moods from the way she's just standing there.

'Sure,' I reply giving in.

'The sooner you leave, the sooner you'll be back,' she says sweetly and subtly ushering me to the door.

'I, um,' I stutter.

'Gracie and I will be fine, won't we?' She says looking up towards my daughter and giving her a friendly smile. A part of my panic melts then and I realise Brenda will be fine with her, probably much better without me in this nervous state making things worse.

'Yes,' Gracie says quietly finally speaking. 'We will be fine.' I stare at them both, telling my feet to move. Finally, they listen and I grab my keys and go.

I rush through the front door. My heart is pounding through my ears, I'm out of breath and most probably very red faced. I was fine until my brain kept taunting me with all the way this could go wrong, which caused me to speed to the shop and back like my life depended on it.

When I walk into the living room, they are just sat there, both in one piece. I am not sure what I was expecting to happen while I was gone. They both look up at me and I'm sure by this point Brenda must be considering my mental stability and perhaps her relationship status. Her warm smile welcomes me, but when I look over to Gracie, her face is expressionless and she looks completely lost.

The Way Back

'Tea?' I ask holding up a carton of milk and a packet of chocolate digestives.

'Go on then,' Brenda says her smile beaming. The two of them are in two completely different and opposite moods.

'Everything ok?' I ask Gracie.

'Yes,' Gracie says coming back to reality after a few seconds, she looks up and forces a smile. 'Not fancying a tea though, I think I'm going to rest my eyes for a bit.' Her tone is almost robotic. She stands up and slowly walks out of the room. I look towards Brenda and she looks just as concerned and confused as me.

'I guess I'll put the kettle on,' I say finally breaking the silence between us. I have no idea what to think so I can only imagine what is going through Brenda's head.

As I stand in the kitchen, waiting for the kettle to boil I can't get the look of Gracie's face out of my head. There was nothing in her face, no emotion at all, like she was somewhere else and far from reality. What does that mean? If she had cried or even shouted, at least I could've reacted. There was no emotion in her, she's given me nothing, how am I supposed to know how to respond to that?

I walk out of the kitchen, tightly clutching the mug handles; the last thing I want is another two stains on the clean carpet. I hear Brenda's voice and when I walk towards it, I see Gracie standing there again.

'Are you ok?' I ask, she looks a little better, her face is more responsive now.

'Er, yes,' she says.

'Did you want a cup of tea then?' I ask not knowing what else to say.

'Er, no. I am going to go and see Andy I think,' she explains, avoiding both mine and Brenda's eye contact. She's barely even looking in our direction.

'Ok,' I reply slowly, debating whether it's a good idea to let her leave the house. Since when were her and Andy talking again?

She walks out before I can protest and I panic that I've done the wrong thing by letting her go. I reassure myself, it's only down the road and it's Andy. It's good that she's finally going to see him. Perhaps she will tell him something we don't know. If she actually is going there. What if she's lying again?

'Are you ok Connor?' Brenda asks, her voice reminds me that she's sitting there and I immediately feel bad for forgetting about her, again, even if it was for a few seconds.

'I don't know why she is acting so strange,' I say giving her an apologetic look and handing her a tea.

'It's ok, it's a weird time, I understand,' she replies. I'm grateful that she's being so understanding but I really dread to think what is going through her head right now.

'What did you talk about while I was gone?' I ask adjusting my tone to avoid myself from sounding like I am accusing her, but she wasn't acting like that before I left.

'I was trying to get to know her, asking her some questions about herself,' she explains, 'but she seemed like she was in a world of her own. She wasn't replying to my questions, she was talking complete nonsense. At one point, she called me Jane.' She looks at me straight in the eyes. 'Who's Jane?'

'What?' I say in shock. 'I know how that sounds but honestly I have no idea,' I explain and her expression softens.

'Have you ever seen her act like that before?' She asks.

'No, I don't think I have ever seen anyone act like that before,' I admit. Since coming back, I have witnessed some odd behaviour from Gracie, mostly mood swings but nothing like this. 'I probably shouldn't have let her leave, called a doctor instead or something.'

'Maybe getting out the house will be good for her, she might have just been overwhelmed, she's been through a lot,' she suggests. Her words are slightly comforting which settles my worry a little. 'Keeping her here may have upset her more.'

'That's true and she is with Andy now, that's good,' I say, telling myself more than I'm telling her. I pull my phone out of my pocket and text Andy to make sure she's there. I stare at my phone waiting for the three dots to turn into a message and feel relief when he confirms. At least she was telling the truth this time.

'Have you ever thought she may be suffering from a brain injury?' Brenda asks after a few quiet seconds. Her comment comes out of nowhere and surprises me. I almost spit my drink out at her bluntness. The thought that something was wrong with her hadn't even crossed my mind.

'Nothing has shown up in any of the scans,' I reply feeling defensive, but I know she isn't saying it as an attack. 'I talk with her doctor regularly, telling her everything that's happening, even the smaller things.' I explain. 'It's all I can think to do to help and hopefully it will.' Brenda reaches out and takes my hand.

'It's ok, we will get through this and she will be fine,' she says giving me a reassuring smile.

7

*

By the next morning Gracie still hasn't come back. Andy texted me to let me know that she was staying the night, but I still felt like I was up most of the night waiting for her to come back. Brenda left early this morning and since then I have been sat here trying to be productive. Although, really, I have just been waiting for her to come back. I need to speak to her and find out what happened yesterday.

'Gracie, you're back,' I say as I hear the front door open. I almost run into the hallway to see her taking her shoes off at the door. She looks up at me with a look that again, is impossible to read.

'Yep,' she says bluntly, picking her shoes up and putting them in the cupboard. Is she angry at me? Why is she speaking to me like that?

'Are you ok?' I ask cautiously.

'Yes,' another short reply.

'Ok, good,' I reply awkwardly. 'It's just that you left so quickly yesterday I was worried.'

'Oh, I just had plans I was late for,' she explains, her eyes are looking everywhere but at me.

'Well Brenda had to leave early this morning, but she will be back soon,' I explain and her stiffness seems to relax a little.

'Ok,' she says simply, her frown loosening.

'Look Gracie, if–'

'It just freaked me out a bit,' she interrupts me finally making eye contact.

'Ok,' I reply slowly, feeling relieved that she's finally giving me a real answer. 'I just want to check though, you're ok with her being here?'

'Uh yeah!' She says enthusiastically, her tone throws me, it's too much and I don't believe it. She's upset, it's so clear but why?

'I'm happy to talk about it if you want to, whenever you want.' I offer.

'Thanks,' she says, finally smiling at me. 'Right now, I think I just want to get in the shower.'

'Ok, no problem,' I reply. She walks past me and up the stairs. 'I'm going to the pub later, so if you want to invite Andy round for some company, that might be a nice idea.'

'Yea, maybe,' she replies sounding completely uninterested.

8

*

The next morning, I stand in the kitchen staring at the table. I woke up early to make breakfast for the three of us. Brenda spent last night here. After my conversation with Gracie yesterday, I realised that she clearly just doesn't know Brenda yet. It was stupid of me to throw her into a situation like that after the past two years she has endured. I should've been a lot more considerate when it came to bringing a stranger into her life. No wonder she left so quickly, she obviously felt uncomfortable. I'm stupid for putting her in that position, but now it's done and the best thing I can do is make sure she now feels safe around Brenda. So I thought this morning, we could have a very chilled out breakfast and let Gracie get to know her. It's seems like a very simple solution.

'The food is all ready now, just waiting on Gracie to wake up,' I explain to Brenda walking back into the bedroom. She is lying in the bed, staring at her phone.

'Ok, great!' She says looking up and smiling at me. 'So, how do you want to do this, do you want me to wait in here?'

'Oh, I haven't even thought about it,' I admit, I hesitate for second. 'If you wait in the kitchen then I could speak to her before?' I suggest. She nods in agreement, putting her phone down on the bedside table.

'Let me quickly change and then I'll see you down there,' she says smiling at me. I nod and walk into the bathroom.

I look in the mirror and smile to myself, Brenda is being amazing through all of this, I really couldn't ask for anyone better to go through this with. Well, one person, my mind wanders and I drag it back. I can't think about her today. I pick up my toothbrush and put it under the tap when I hear Brenda's voice.

'Sorry what?' I say walking back into the bedroom.

'Gracie,' I hear Brenda's voice just outside the bedroom. I follow it and see her standing there, 'anyone in there?' She says, turning to look at me, she gives me a worried look. I look down the hallway to see Gracie standing there.

'Gracie?' I say trying to get her attention. She is just standing there outside her room, clutching the door frame. She has a misty look in her eyes, her face has gone completely white and her whole body is shaking. Before I can get to her, she falls face first onto the floor.

The bright, artificial hospital lights are starting to hurt my eyes. I've been waiting far too long for someone to speak to me and now I am starting to worry. I sent Brenda off to get us some food and coffee and she still isn't back. It feels like I have been waiting hours to hear something. I check my watch, it's been two hours since we got to the hospital. I pick up my phone to see if Penny has answered me. My battery is low, probably because I have been checking every two minutes for her reply ever since I sent the message an hour ago. Why isn't Penny here? I need her here. What could she be doing that would make her take so long to reply to me?

I look down the hallway hoping she will suddenly appear. I stand up immediately when I see a familiar face approaching me.

'Hello Connor,' she says giving me a friendly smile. It's Gracie's doctor, the one I have been keeping in touch about Gracie's symptoms. She's dressed casually, not in her usual doctor attire, she must have been called in.

'Hi,' I say weakly. 'How is she?'

She hesitates for a second and I feel all the blood rush to my face.

'She thinks she was shot,' she finally says.

'What!' I exclaim. Shot? How could she think that? My mind tries to think of a logical explanation. 'That's crazy, do you think she is lying?' I ask.

'No,' she says simply. 'I think she thinks she got shot.'

'What do you mean?'

'I think it was an hallucination and I don't think that this is the first time she has experienced something like this either.'

'What!' I say again. 'No, surely not. I would've noticed.'

'To notice, you'd have to have be inside her head,' she says.

'I, uh,' I'm lost for words. None of this makes any sense, it would be obvious if she were – suddenly I think back to the way she was behaving the other day when she met Brenda, could that? Was she then? It would explain her behaviour but no, it couldn't have been.

'I have been keeping track of Gracie,' she says dragging me out of thought. I look up at her. 'I've taken into consideration all you have been telling me, everything that has happened.'

'Right,' I say, feeling worry gather in the back of my throat.

'She's showing signs of having a dual personality. It explains the memory loss and the mood swings, as for the hallucinations, they may have been caused by PTSD.'

'No way,' I say feeling defensive, 'I would've definitely noticed that!'

'Dual personalities tend to mimic the behaviour of their main identity, so it can be really difficult to notice,' she explains. 'Gracie may have developed a second personality to cope with the environment she was in when she went missing, that would explain why she doesn't remember being there.'

'What about her memory loss now?' I ask.

'I couldn't say,' she explains. 'I have theories, but I couldn't give you a definite answer, at least not right now.'

'Right,' I say, none of this feels real. 'Am I allowed to go and see her?'

'Yes, but it's vital you are cautious with this information. Due to the nature of that environment, we must be cautious with the second personality. Also, Gracie may not know about the personality and that can be very distressing to someone when they find out,' she warns.

'I understand,' I say nodding.

'Ok,' she says. 'I'll show you to her room.'

I follow her through the corridors in silence. How could this be true? Gracie is my daughter, I would've known if it wasn't her, I am sure of it.

When I am pointed to the door, I walk in sheepishly not knowing what to expect. Gracie is lying on the bed with her eyes closed, just like when I first saw her a few weeks ago. I suddenly feel defeated that we're back at square one. I slowly walk into the room and stand next to the bed.

'Gracie,' I say softly, she opens her eyes and looks up at me.

'She shot me,' she whispers breathlessly.

'No Gracie, you collapsed.' I explain.

'No,' she whispers.

'This might come as a shock to you, but we think it was a hallucination.'

'It felt so real,' she argues, her voice breaks as she struggles to speak.

'I know it did, but you're ok, you weren't shot,' I say slowly.

She sits up in the bed, pulling her blanket off her. She looks down at her body, pulling her jumper up, revealing her stomach. She stares at it for a few seconds before slowly putting her hand on her skin.

'Since you came back, we have been monitoring you and I have been speaking with doctors. We've been discussing your blackouts, your behaviour and all the things you have experienced since you came back,' I explain, choosing my words carefully.

'And,' she says impatiently, she is desperate for answers. I can't keep the truth from her, this is about her, it's happening to her, it's unfair to be keeping her in the dark.

154

'Gracie, they have diagnosed you with a dual personality disorder,' I explain.

'What?' Her voice trembles.

'You experienced a massive amount of trauma when you went missing and this is how you coped with it, but we can help you.' I reassure her.

'I don't understand,' she says.

'It's ok, I know it's confusing, but the doctor will be able to talk you through it and explain it.' My heart is breaking looking at her. She looks so sad and so helpless. For a moment she's in her own head, I let her stay there to give her the chance to at least try and make sense of what I've told her. So, I wait for her to say something else.

Brenda appears in the doorway; I turn around and smile at her. 'Thank God you're ok Gracie,' she says smiling at my daughter. 'Connor, I am just going outside to make a phone call, I just wanted to let you know that I am back. No sign of Penny yet though,' she explains.

'Thanks Brenda,' I say smiling appreciatively at her. I can't believe Penny is still not here, this really isn't like her at all. I turn around to look at Gracie, she's staring at Brenda, looking surprised. Maybe I shouldn't have brought her here with me. Before I can defend or explain myself, she looks back at me.

'I know I should have so many questions,' Gracie says, 'but I feel like my brain is completely scrambled, I'm so hungry, am I allowed to eat?' She asks. Her answer surprises me but it's almost a relief to hear something so normal come out of her mouth.

'Yes,' I say, feeling slightly relieved she didn't say anything about Brenda being here. 'I think getting some food into your system is a good idea.'

'Would you mind getting me a sandwich and a drink please?'

'There is some orange juice here,' I say reaching to the table next to her and picking up a plastic jug. She looks at it and scrunches up her nose.

'Erm, I don't really want that,' she says, 'can you get me something else please?'

'No problem,' I say standing up, I reach over and kiss her on the forehead.

She smiles weakly at me as I walk out of the room. I know I shouldn't but part of me feels good after speaking to her. She seemed more than ok and I have hope that she will get better. I quickly rush to the lift when I see the doors open and press the button for the ground floor.

When the doors open on the ground floor, I walk out looking up at the signs on the wall, looking for the arrow pointing to the shop.

'That way,' a voice says and I turn around to see Gracie's doctor again.

'Oh hi,' I laugh, 'I'm just getting Gracie a sandwich, she said she was hungry, that's a good sign, isn't it?'

'Yes,' she agrees, 'hunger is a very good sign'.

'Good, she seems to be ok.' I explain, 'she took the information well I think'.

She turns and gives me an odd look. 'She took what information well?' She asks slowly.

'About her diagnoses,' I explain. 'I know I wasn't supposed to tell her bu—'

'No, Connor, you shouldn't have told her,' she interrupts me. 'How did you know it was Gracie you were talking to?'

'I uh, I just knew, she's my daughter,' I say defending my actions.

'We need to go back, now,' she says, her eyes are wide and her face looks panicked. She starts pressing the lift buttons frantically. 'I'm serious.'

Louie

Louie

1

*

'Fuck off! You don't care about me; you're just going to do what you want anyway,' I shout standing up and storming out the house. 'I hate you.'

The last words I said to her haunt me every day. I was so cold, so rude and if I had known I wasn't going to see her again, I wouldn't have said it. I was just so mad at her, so hurt with the way she was treating me.

The moment I heard she was back, I had to see her with my own eyes. The last two years had been hell for me. I had no idea where she was, who she was with or even if she was safe. I knew that Gracie could handle herself, but I also knew she underestimated what the world could throw at her.

I wasn't surprised when I found out she had gone missing, I knew she was going to go at some point. I'll admit I didn't expect it so soon, a part of me thought I would be able to convince her to stay. She would talk about leaving all the time, how one day she would be free, free to finally be who she wanted to be; whatever that meant.

Standing here right now, in front of her house is fucking scary. I'm nervous to see her, scared of what's going to be on the other side of the door. I really thought she would've tried to contact me, at least now that she's back. What if she doesn't want to see me? And that's why she hasn't tried to call. Before I can wimp out anymore, I reach out and press the doorbell. My heart starts to pound even faster now and I can feel my cheeks getting hotter.

The door flies open. And it's her on the other side. It's Gracie. I feel some kind of relief seeing her, seeing that she's safe.

'Hello trouble,' I say feeling the smile grow on my face.

She stares back at me blankly and I start to get a weird feeling. Why is she looking at me like that? Something isn't right, I can feel it. What the fuck is going on here? Before I can say anything to her, the door opens wider and Andy appears behind her. Of course, he's here. Nothing is ever easy with Gracie.

'Louie,' Andy says, his eyes digging into mine, warning me. I can tell that he's definitely not happy to see me. He's giving me that look that I've seen so many times before, the *'stay away from Gracie or else'* look. Or else what? He's never followed through with any of his warnings; apart from that time he punched me in the face, but even that was a pathetic attempt. 'She doesn't know who you are, she doesn't remember,' Andy explains.

She doesn't remember what? I look towards Gracie, hoping to see her smirking, something that tells **me** that she's lying and this is all one big trick on Andy, but she just stares hnrk at mo blankly. There is nothing in her face that indicates what Andy is saying is true. Could she have really forgotten everything? Is that why she's back?

'Surely Gracie can speak for herself,' I say winking at her and trying to recover from the bombshell Andy has just dropped. It can't be true. Gracie isn't the girl who loses her memory. I stare at her face, hoping she will give me any kind of sign that shows me that she's still in there. 'Do you remember me? I ask keeping my eyes on her and ignoring Andy behind her.

'No,' she says weakly after the longest second of my life. She can't even look me in the eye now. Everything about this feels weird, I have never seen her like this before, she's so timid and shy. It's so unlike her. Something isn't right, I can feel it. I need to speak to her alone, without Andy lurking behind her.

'It's been a while, I'd love a catch up,' I say, gesturing for her to come out and sit with me. I'm trying to play it cool but in reality, I am completely freaked out by the way she is acting right now.

'I, uh,' she hesitates nervously, so unsure of herself. What the fuck has happened to her?

'You'd think a person who lost their memory would do everything they could to find out about their old life and I was part of that life,' I say, surely, she can't say no to that?

'Gracie, you don't have to listen to him,' Andy pipes up and Gracie flinches. She actually flinches at the sound of his voice. I look up at Andy, suddenly feeling very suspicious of him. I wait patiently for her to respond. When her eyes finally meet mine, I try to give her a reassuring smile. She nods slowly, it's barely noticeable. I walk away and take a seat on the bench outside her house.

'Gracie if you could just remember, you would know he's bad news!' Andy shouts, his voice sounds desperate. Remember? Remember what? Andy doesn't know what happened between Gracie and I, let alone remember it. He must only know what she told him at the time and I can only imagine how far from the truth that was.

I watch as Gracie slowly steps out the house and closes the door behind her. Just the way she's moving is so weird. It's hard to see that she's acting this strange around me, she is very clearly uncomfortable and I have no idea why. I hate this! She sits down next to me, leaving a very obvious gap between us. I have never seen her like this before, it's caught me completely off guard. I don't know what I was expecting when I found out she was back, but it definitely wasn't this.

'I can't believe your back,' I say finding my voice again. She doesn't say anything so I carry on. 'I've been wanting to come and see you ever since I heard.' I look up at her and she's staring back at me blankly. Seemingly completely uninterested by me. Again, she doesn't say anything. 'Where did you go?' I ask.

'I don't know, I don't remember,' she mumbles her eyes reaching for the floor again. It's like she can't even look me in the eye. I can't stand to look at her like this, I can't sit here and watch this empty shell version of Gracie.

'I don't have much time,' I explain looking at my watch, 'but I would really like to talk to you some more, can I take you to lunch tomorrow?' I ask. I want her alone, there's something wrong here. I need answers and I can just tell that this isn't the time for getting any.

'I'm not really sure what I'm doing tomorrow,' she says, politely excusing herself.

'Great, I'll come by at 12 to pick you up,' I say completely ignoring her lame excuse, she doesn't even protest or complain. She just accepts it. This isn't Gracie at all.

2

*

As I stand in the queue, waiting to order for us, I feel completely overwhelmed. Today, I picked up Gracie and brought her here, to one of the cafes in our town. I turn around and look over to where I left her. She picked a table by the window and now she's sat down, staring outside and watching the world go by. I don't know what has happened, but today I picked up a completely different person. Gracie turns away from the window and her eyes search the room, she finds me and looks straight at me. Her eyes force themselves onto mine and her mouth lifts up into a cheeky grin. I forgot how much of an effect that smile had on me. It's as if she can read my mind because her eyes light up. This is the Gracie that left me two years ago.

What could've possibly happened in the last 24 hours for her to have changed that drastically? Was it all fake? A show for Andy? I don't know what the fuck is going on but I am going to find out. Our relationship may have been a secret but that doesn't mean it never happened. I feel a pull in the back of my throat, that tiny bit of doubt. If it's really true that Gracie doesn't remember her old life, then that means that the only person who knows about us, is me.

'Is that Gracie?' The waitress says to me as it's my turn to be served. No hello or how are you? Customer service at its finest there.

'It is,' I say recognising her face from school. I start to tell her our order but notice that she's barely paying any attention to me. Finally, she starts to slowly tap our order onto the screen, fully distracted by Gracie's presence in the café. I pull out my wallet from my back pocket and wait for the machine to light up. I take a quick glance back at Gracie, to check she's still there and I see that she is still staring at me, still giving me that look.

'I can't believe she's back,' the waitress says tapping the screen, I tap my card against the machine and place it back into my wallet. The news of Gracie's return has spread around this small town and everyone is talking about it. When we walked into the café, everyone's eyes were on her, even walking down the street she was causing a distraction. 'And here with you,' the waitress adds. I look up at her and scowl.

'Well, we can't all have a stick up our arse, like you.' I reply, picking up our drinks and walking away. Fucking bitch. She stands there with her mouth open, perhaps that'll teach her to keep her fucking mouth shut. Her comment doesn't surprise me though; no one really knows the truth. In their eyes, I am the bad guy. The one who got between the two childhood sweethearts, perfect Gracie and innocent Andy. Ugh. I fucking hate Andy. Such a fucking pussy. I hate that everyone thought she was his, but that couldn't have been further from the truth. Gracie was mine.

The Way Back

About six months before Gracie went missing, we started seeing each other. Well, she started seeing me. It happened so quickly. It was a weird relationship; so fucked up! She was so hot and cold with me and it sent me up the wall. I didn't expect her to drag me in the way she did, but she was so different from any girl before. When we were alone, she would be all over me but in public it was as if I didn't exist. It made me want her so much more. She never wanted Andy to find out, to be honest I couldn't understand why she was even with him because she made it very clear that she hated him. We would spend hours bitching about him, laughing about all the things he would say or do. He was a joke and so was their relationship. It was a weird situation, but admittedly, it was addictive too. When I thought I finally had her, the next day she would be back with him, claiming to him that he was the only one. Only I knew the truth. At first, it was all fun and games and I liked to play. But then I fell for her.

'A vanilla latte for you,' I say putting it down in front of her. She smiles as I sit down on the chair opposite. Her eyes are still on mine and it's starting to freak me out a bit. I distract myself by pouring my tea. She silently watches me.

'You seem different today,' I point out picking up my drink. She mimics me by picking up her coffee and takes a sip. Seeing her like this is reassuring, I was really starting to worry that I'd lost her.

'I feel different,' she gives me a mischievous smile and puts her coffee back down on the table. She gives me that amused look of, I know something you don't. What a fucking little tease! We sit in silence, her last words lingering in the air.

'I was sorry to hear about your mum,' I say sadly, changing the subject.

'Thanks,' she replies and her smile falls. I feel bad for making her sad, but I just wanted to say it, acknowledge it and let her know that I was thinking about her when it happened. I lose her for a second while her mind goes somewhere else, maybe I shouldn't have said anything but I want her to know that I'm here and always have been. I think that was the problem last time.

'So, crazy stuff you coming back after all this time, we thought you were a goner,' I say trying to bring her back, lighten the mood and tempt a reaction from her, or at least a smile.

'Insane,' she says, a grin spreads on her face and I can feel my smile fighting to come out. She dips her spoon into her drink with her eyes still locked on mine. I watch as she slowly takes the spoon out of her coffee and puts it into her mouth. She knows what she's doing right now and even though it's fucking sexy, I can't let her distract me. I need her to admit to me that she remembers.

'You know before you went missing, you and I used to spend a lot of time with each other,' I say, studying her face for any kind of recognition.

'Oh really?' She says simply.

'Yes. I remember you were always playing games, getting caught up in little lies,' I laugh. 'You weren't the perfect little angel that Andy thought you were, that everyone thought you were.' I tease, knowing exactly how to push her buttons.

'Louie, just say what you want to say, I'm not playing games.' She says rolling her eyes, clearly irritated by my comment. I knew the mention of Andy would piss her off, it always has.

'Ha ha, ok,' I say stopping the act. It's definitely her and she remembers. That gross feeling in my stomach finally starts to ease. 'You finally got out then? I knew you would, I just didn't think you'd come back so soon.'

'I ran into some complications,' she explains.

'Care to expand on that?' I ask.

'Not really,' she says quietly. I try to hide my disappointment, I guess she doesn't trust me with that information anymore.

'Well, it's good to see you, I missed you,' I admit. Even after all the shit she put me through, it's still feels so good to see her.

'When are you going to dump him and be with me,'
I moan. 'I'm sick of seeing you together, holding his
scrawny hand and him acting like you're his, when you're
actually mine.'

'I don't belong to either of you,' she replies
bluntly, rolling onto her back and away from me. Maybe
bringing Andy up right now wasn't the best idea, it had just
been bugging me all day. That smug bastard.

'What would happen if I told him about our little
affair,' I tease, although I have thought about telling him.
At least then I'd have her all to myself, there would be no
more secrets. If anything, I would be doing her a favour. It
seems as though she hates him as much as I do. It makes no
sense. Her face completely changes, the look she gives me
sends a chill down my spine.

'That would be your mistake,' she says looking me
dead in the eyes. 'And your loss,' she threatens.

'Ok,' I say softly, trying to break some of the
tension I have just created. 'But is it really wrong for me to
just want you all to myself? I hate it when you pretend you
don't know me.' I think back to the day before. She walked
straight past me, hand in hand with Andy. The look she
gave me, made me sick.

'Louie, it's complicated. You know I can't explain
it to you and you knew that from the beginning,' she says
sounding irritated. I hate that she holds that over me. Yes, I
agreed to it in the beginning but I didn't realise it was

going to feel like this. I didn't think I would actually fall in love with her. 'But just know, it's you, only you, ok?' Her voice softens.

'You sometimes act like that, even when we're alone,' I add. 'I never know where I stand with you, I feel like I am always waiting for you to make the first move.' I say, cringing at how pathetic I am sounding right now. I can't help it though; this is what she's doing to me.

'Isn't that part of the fun?' She winks at me.

I hate how she does that, how she knows exactly what to say to make me forget. I nod and roll on top of her, balancing my weight so I don't squash her. She lets me close to her and everything feels better. I lightly tickle her; just needing to hear her laugh. She squeals loudly and I cringe knowing her dad is in the house. If he found us, then this would all be over. I lean down and kiss her slowly.

'Say it again,' I whisper.

'It's only you,' she whispers back into my ear. If only that was true.

The chips I ordered are placed in front of me, pulling me out of my thoughts. I look up to say thanks and realise it's that nosey bitch from before. She gives me a fake smile and looks towards Gracie.

Gracie looks up when she realises that the waitress is staring at her. A few awkward seconds pass before

171

Gracie snaps aggressively. 'Take a picture, it will last longer.' The waitress flinches before recovering and walking away. I try to hide my amusement, serves her right for being so self-righteous.

'So,' I say trying to get back to my point, 'it was weird seeing you yesterday, you didn't seem like yourself at all, it–'

'It wasn't me,' she interrupts me, her comment is so simple but completely throws me.

'What, you're saying it wasn't you?' I ask slowly, repeating what she said back to her.

'I'm saying it wasn't the Gracie you thought,' she clarifies, but that hasn't helped at all. She is still talking absolute nonsense.

'Did I speak to you yesterday?' I ask slowly, still trying to understand what's going on.

'Technically, no,' she replies looking satisfied. What on earth is she going on about? It sounds like she's implying that I was speaking to someone else and not her.

'What? Like there is two of you?' I sound like I've completely lost the plot, but that's what she is insinuating right now.

'Something like that,' she shrugs. Is she playing a game with me? If she is, I am completely out of my depth this time.

'Have we met before?' I ask, trying to think of the right questions to ask. Each answer she gives me, makes me even more confused.

'Yes, of course! Like you said, we've had some pretty good times,' she winks at me. What on earth? She takes one last sip of her coffee before looking up at me. I have so many more questions with no idea where to start. Is this all a game? But what would be the point? I reach out and grab her hand.

'Gracie,' I say softly. 'No more jokes, please tell me what's going on.' For just a second her face softens and I think she's going to open up.

'I've got to dash,' she says quickly, her walls shoot up. Before I can say anything else, she stands up and pulls her coat off the back of the chair, 'see you later'. What the fuck? There is no way in hell I am letting her leave like this.

'Wait!' I shout, standing up and chasing her out of the café. She turns around and looks at me expectantly. Every single question I had suddenly goes out of my brain and I realise all I want in this moment is for her to stay. 'Do you need help again?' I ask, it's the first thing I can think to say. For a split second, she looks vulnerable and I realise that whatever is going on here, it's even bigger than her.

'Gracie's a catch,' she pauses for a second. 'You should get her back, keep her safe and away from Andy.'

What does that even mean? Has she gone completely mad? Why is she talking about herself like that? She uses my confusion as an escape, before I can even comprehend her words, she's gone.

I walk back into the café and sit back down in my chair. There are people staring at me, probably because they have just watched me chase the missing girl outside, but my brain is too full to care. Gracie's words, everything she's just said is whizzing around in my brain. She's playing a game with me; she has to be.

3

*

Gracie is fucking with me, I know it! But I can't get over that look of fear on her face yesterday. That was real and even though it only lasted a second, I can tell somethings going on. And today, I intend to find out.

> 'Gracie's a catch, you should get her back, keep her safe and away from Andy.'

Her odd request lingers in my brain. Fine, I'll play along. I knock firmly on her front door. I look around and see there is no car in the drive, which means her dad is probably at work. That's a good thing, he hates me. I wait patiently as I hear someone on the other side of the door, fiddling with the locks. The door finally opens, revealing Gracie.

I smile and in response, she slams the door in my face. I react quickly by putting my foot in the way. The door hits my foot hard and I bravely hide the seething pain of having a door slammed on your foot.

'That's not very polite,' I point out. What the fuck was that?

'I have no interest in speaking to you,' she says, looking down at the floor. She's nervous, but why? What kind of game is this?

'Well, what have I done to receive this welcome?' I ask. She's gone back to how she was the other day, all timid and claiming memory loss I assume. 'Surely nothing that you can remember,' I smirk. Her face reacts too quickly for her to control it.

'Why are you here?' She asks bluntly. Wow, she really isn't happy to see me. This is weird. Surely after two years, we can't be going back to this hot and cold shit. We're adults now.

'I want a chance with you, again.' I say, remembering the instructions Gracie gave me to her little game.

'I'm not interested,' she says quickly, still unable to make eye contact with me.

'I know the truth about everything,' I warn. Well, I know that something is going on and since Gracie doesn't seem to be playing by the rules, I won't be either. I am going to get to the bottom of this and if that means chatting shit to get there, I am more than happy to do so.

'You're bluffing,' she mumbles weakly. Well, that was pathetic. I don't think I have ever seen her back down that easily. Is this part of the game?

'Do you really want to test that theory?' I ask. She looks down at the floor again. What is this? I wonder. Why is she acting this way? It's pathetic. 'This isn't really about memory loss, is it?' I continue my bluff.

'What do you want?' She asks backing down, that was too easy.

'I want another chance!' I say simply. 'With you, without Andy getting in the way.' I add, remembering Gracie's last request.

'Andy isn't in the way anymore anyway,' she says after a few seconds, looking even more pathetic.

'Perfect!' I say. 'So...'

'Would you like to come in?' She weakly steps to the side, inviting me to walk in.

'I'd love to!' I smile, stepping into the house. I stop in front of her and look down at her. She can't even look up at me, her hands are balled into anxious fists and her whole posture is just small. I put my hand under her chin and lift her face up to look at me. There's nothing in her eyes.

I feel my gut drop. I don't know who the fuck this is, but it's not my Gracie...

4

*

I lie sprawled out on Gracie's sofa staring at the TV. It's been a few days since Gracie tasked me in babysitting the BTEC version of her. I've spent every day here this week and there has been no sign of the real Gracie. I know it sounds crazy and I still don't know how any of this is possible, but I know for sure that whoever that person is, it's not Gracie. It just can't be.

I've been dying to see Gracie, but every time I come over, it always that fucking freak who's pretending to be her. I feel like she's hiding from me. I'm trying really hard to be understanding but none of this makes any fucking sense. I have done everything she has asked me to do. I have kept her safe, whatever that means and I've made sure that Andy has stayed away. I groan loudly in frustration as the living room door opens. All the light rushes into the room, putting a glare on the TV screen. I look up and see her standing at the door.

'Gracie,' I complain.

'Yes,' she answers.

'You're letting the light in, shut the door,' I say rudely. I sit up and watch as she walks back to the door and closes it softly. Yep, that's still not Gracie. There is no way she would let me speak to her like that.

I'm still struggling with the idea that there is two of them. There's still a small part of me that thinks Gracie is playing some kind of game with me. But surely by now she would be taking it too far? What would be the point? I have no idea what is going on, or how any of this is possible, but the more time I spend with this person the surer I am that it's not her. She couldn't be this good at playing a game, could she? All I know is that there's somehow two of them.

Yesterday I realised that I really hate this version of Gracie, if that's even the right word? She is so boring and annoying. Sometimes when I speak to her, it's actually like speaking to a brick wall, one of those plain ones, with nothing to look at. There is no personality in her whatsoever. She just stares back at me blankly all the time, like the lights are on but there's no one home.

'What?' I spit when I notice her staring at me again. She's always fucking staring at me. I'm pissed off that I haven't seen Gracie since the café, how could she just drop a bombshell like that and leave me here to just deal with it? I have so many questions but there is no point in asking that air head over there. Gracie's just left me here to babysit and it's annoying that she's not even showed her face, even after I have done what she told me to do.

'Nothing,' she says shrugging her shoulders. I still can't get over how much this imposter looks like Gracie. She's identical, in appearance. Two years ago, Gracie would never tell me why she was leaving, could this be the reason why? But where is Gracie now?

'We're going to the pub tonight,' I tell her shoving a handful of crisps into my mouth. This is my plan to draw Gracie in.

'Erm.'

'We're going to the pub tonight,' I repeat. 'You don't want me to tell everyone your little secret, do you?' I warn. I'm still not sure what this so-called *'secret'* is but threatening her with it is working a treat.

'I didn't say no,' she replies backing out of the living room and leaving me on my own.

My plan is to take her out tonight because I know that there is no way Gracie would let this idiot leave the house, not if she wants to keep this a secret. No one will believe it's her, surely. She has got to make an appearance tonight; she can't hide forever.

I sigh, rolling onto my side, I hope that I'm right about that. I look over at the blue armchair in the corner of the room. I smile to myself; it makes me think of Gracie and takes my mind to somewhere in the past.

'Quickly now,' Gracie says dragging me into the living room.

'What are we doing?' I ask as she pushes me down on the armchair.

'What do you think we're doing,' she says sarcastically, leaning down to kiss me.

'Is anyone here?' I ask, cautiously.

'No, not at the moment,' she smiles cheekily at me, sitting down on my lap and straddling around my legs. She leans in and kisses me again. All caution goes out the window, she's been so cold with me recently, I don't know when I'll get another chance to kiss her like this again. I grab her hips and pull her closer to me. She pulls her top over her head. I reach up and start kissing her neck. Her skin feels so good on my lips. I feel her tugging on my jeans as I unbutton hers.

'I'm going to miss this,' she mumbles into me as I push my hand into her jeans.

'You don't have to,' I whisper, biting her skin. She ignores me and carries on kissing me, pushing her body even closer to mine. 'You don't have to go,' I repeat myself, pulling away from her.

'Why do you always have to ruin the mood?' She says sitting up and frowning.

'You started it,' I argue feeling myself getting angry.

'Ugh, I'm sick of this conversation,' she says pulling away and standing up. 'To be honest I didn't realise it was open for discussion,' she adds, buttoning her jeans and picking up her top from the floor. She slips her top back on, opens the living room door and walks out. I stand up and chase after her.

Louie

'Don't walk away from me,' I shout after her. She
turns around and I grab her wrist.

'Let go of me Louie,' she warns.

'Why can't you just let me love you, let us have a
normal relationship.' I shout. 'Why do you want to leave so
bad?'

'It's too complicated for that, you don't get it.' Her
eyes start to fill up.

'Then explain, please.' I loosen my grip on her
wrist, she looks up at me but doesn't say anything. 'I love
you; you can trust me.' She takes a step forward, placing
her hand into mine and looks up at me.

'No,' she says quietly and frustration overcomes
me.

'Gracie, if you don't tell me then I'll tell your
parents that you're going to leave,' I threaten. I don't want
to do this, I don't want to blackmail her, but she's giving
me no choice. She can't leave.

'Go ahead, but either way, you'll lose me.' She
says, her threat is much bigger than mine. I feel my
stomach drop and any last hope of keeping her here goes.
She smiles ever so slightly, making me realise that she's
won and I am always going to be the loser.

The front door opens and she flinches, taking a step away
from me.

'What's going on here?' Gracie's dad asks walking into the house.

'Nothing,' Gracie says quietly. 'Louie, you should go,' she says looking up at me, her voice changing instantly.

'Yes, you should,' Andy says barging into the house before I can say anything else.

I look over to Gracie and she's giving me a blank expression. There's no indication that she wants me to stay, that she even cares. Any emotion she was just showing, has gone now. It's as if she just turns off when anyone else walks into the room. I give her one more second, one more chance to stop me, but she doesn't.

'Fine,' I say quietly after a few seconds. I feel Andy's eyes on me as I walk past him.

'What was that all about?' I hear Andy's voice as I walk out.

'Nothing, it was nothing,' Gracie says bluntly.

'Please, Gracie just talk to me,' Andy begs.

The front door shuts, blocking me out of her life again. If only they knew the truth of what was really going on, maybe I wouldn't be the bad guy all the time.

'I'm going to get some milk,' her voice grabs my attention and my eyes focus back into reality. Before I can answer, she shuts the door, leaving me alone again. I sit up as I hear the front door shut, that was kind of rude! Fuck, I'm not supposed to leave her on her own, I quickly stand up to follow her when I realise, for the first time, I am alone in this house…

She'll be fine.

After looking around the whole house, I find nothing. I don't even know what I was looking for, but I just needed some confirmation that I'm not going crazy or something that tells me at the very least that Gracie isn't messing with me. There's nothing. I walk down the stairs feeling defeated, I needed something, anything to make me feel sane. As I reach the bottom of the stairs, I see her dad's office door open. I wonder if it would be too far to look in. The door is open and is basically inviting me in. There's no harm in checking.

I have never been in here before, it's much smaller than I thought it would be. It's a small space with room for just a bookshelf and a desk. The bookshelf is filled to the brim with books and the desk is messy; I didn't think Gracie's dad would be this unorganised. I walk over to the desk, scanning it. My eyes freeze over a pile of papers with Gracie's name on the first page. This could be something. I pick it up and start flicking through the pages.

It's a file, full of information about Gracie going missing, the medication she is taking and symptoms she is experiencing. As I look through, I see a page with a list of symptoms. One section describes how Gracie is experiencing chunks of memory loss, forgetting things that happen during the day. I read through the list of items, only minor things, until I see my name *'lunch with Louie'*. She forgot she went to lunch with me? Interesting. That would m—

The printer comes to life, making me jump out of my skin. I quickly return the paper back to the desk and walk out. This is what I needed; this is proof. Gracie 2.0 wouldn't remember having lunch because it wasn't her. This is really happening, whatever this is.

A few hours later, I'm sitting in the kitchen scrolling through my phone. There are so many people online using Gracie coming back as an excuse for getting likes and it's so annoying. She would hate this! I look up and see Gracie 2.0 standing at the sink, rinsing some mugs from earlier and staring blankly out of the window. The rest of the afternoon was spent mostly watching TV, the usual babysitting activities. When she got back from the shop, she went upstairs for a short while before joining me back in the living room, we mostly sat in silence, I really don't have any interest in speaking to her.

'I got us some milk,' Gracie's dad says walking into the kitchen. As soon as he clocks me sitting at the kitchen table, I see disappointment wash over his face. He doesn't even smile at me. He hates me, I mean I don't blame him, I can only imagine the poison Andy has filled his head with about me. I would hate me too if any of it was true.

'Gracie already got some,' I point out, just to let my presence in the room known to him.

'No, I didn't,' she says looking at me as if I've just pushed her nan down the stairs. What is she on about? She went out earlier to get milk, she even made me a coffee with it.

'Yes, you did,' I say slowly. What the fuck is she on about? Gracie's dad walks across the kitchen and we both watch as he opens the fridge door.

'Seems like you did,' he says pulling out a carton of milk. I see her face change, she genuinely looks confused, how does she not remember getting it? It was like two hours ago. The room goes silent and everything suddenly feels so weird. She looks over to Gracie's dad and he looks concerned. Am I missing something? 'Don't worry Gracie, you're suffering from memory loss, things like this are bound to happen,' he says.

Well, it can't be because of the memory loss because said memory loss doesn't exist. What the fuck is happening right now? And then it hits me. Oh my god! She was here. Gracie was here. She came into the living room, she spoke to me and I missed it. I have been waiting days and I missed it, just like that. How many times has it been her and I've not realised? Why didn't she say anything?

'Anyway, ya freak, I'm off,' I say hiding my anger and breaking the silence in the room. 'I'll see you later,' I need to get out of here before I flip out. How could she just appear and not say anything?

When we arrive at the pub, it's the same as when we went into the café. All eyes are on her. We walk straight to the bar and I can hear everyone whispering as we walk past. I don't ask her what she wants. If she wants to pretend to be Gracie, then she can drink her usual.

As soon as I picked her up, I could tell straight away it wasn't Gracie. I really thought she'd make an appearance tonight, but clearly not. I can't believe she didn't come. And now, I am stuck babysitting this freak on a Friday night.

I pick up my drink and walk over to my friends. They're sat on a table by the door. She doesn't follow me and just stands at the bar by herself looking like a lost and pathetic little puppy. Suit yourself, it doesn't bother me. She's not the girl I want sitting next to me anyway.

'Back from the dead,' one of the boys say as I sit down.

'The poor girl lived through hell and ended up with you,' my best friend Jack says nudging my arm playfully. He's the only one out of these idiots I actually like. The rest of them are dicks.

'Very funny,' I say taking a sip from my drink. It's not.

The conversation changes to something else that I don't care about. I never usually come out but I thought this was a good excuse to try and lure Gracie out from wherever she's hiding. It didn't and now I'm pissed off.

'Do you really want her to be speaking to Gracie,' Jack says quietly in my ear.

I look up to see who he's talking about. Dianne. She's standing there chatting to Tweedledum. Ahh fuck! Dianne is a girl who used to go to our school, a girl Gracie absolutely despised. It's common knowledge that Gracie came back with *'no memory'*, so I can only imagine the shit Dianne is spirting out of her mouth right now. More proof that this isn't Gracie, there is no way she would let Dianne stand there and speak to her.

I sigh and stand up. Gracie would kill me if she found out Dianne was talking to her clone, I am sure this comes under her list of things to keep her away from. I quickly stride towards the bar and reach out and pull her towards me and away from Dianne.

'Shut up and mind your own business Dianne,' I spit aggressively. Dianne of course pulls a hurt face, making herself look like the victim in this situation. Fuck this. Watching this idiot is starting to feel like a full-time job.

'Why did you pull me away?' She asks, now playing into her victim role as I pull her outside. She looks at me as if I'm crazy, as if I'm the bad one. I'm literally doing her a favour by pulling her away.

'Because that girl is horrible, she is just trying to cause trouble, I don't like you talking to her!' I warn, knowing that I'm trying to reason with an idiot. She doesn't get it, to her I just look like a dick head.

'Why?' She asks.

'It doesn't matter why!' I say trying to hide my irritation. 'Let's go back inside and you can sit with me,' I say, trying to be nice. It's painful. I reach out and gently pull her towards me.

'No. I'd rather go home,' she says so quietly, I can barely hear it. So pathetic.

'Come on,' I say starting to get impatient.

'No!' She says, much louder now. Wow look who's grown some big girl balls. I pull on her wrist as I start to lose the little patience I had. She pulls back harshly, so I let go and she falls back onto the floor landing on her bum.

I stare down at her feeling like a dickhead. Fuck this! Gracie is starting to take the piss now. She can't even show up once. Actually, she can and when she does, she doesn't even acknowledge me. I'm pissed off. Why am I even doing this? I'm standing here on a Friday night looking like a fucking fool.

'Suit yourself,' I say. I don't care if she goes home, in fact I would rather her go. I turn around and walk away. Either she will follow me or not, but I don't care anymore. I'm done with this shit! I should've known it was going to be something like this and should have never got back involved with her. I walk back inside and back to my table.

'Where is Gracie?' Jack asks.

'She's gone to powder her nose, or some other girl shit,' I say staring at the door and waiting for her to come back.

5

*

I wake up on the sofa the next morning to the sound of someone banging on the front door. I sit up and look around, feeling the noise pound through my brain. I'm in the living room, the rest of the house is quiet. I must be the only person here. I don't remember getting home last night.

I stand up and rub the sleep out of my eyes. The knocking carries on. Jesus. Someone is eager for me to answer. I walk towards the door half expecting to see that Hermes wanker. Part of me hopes that it's Gracie coming to bollock me for leaving her dumb counterpart to fend for herself last night. At least I'd actually get to see her, even if it's because she's angry with me. I open the door and squint as the sun light attacks me.

'Andy,' I say almost surprised to see him. He's looking at me as if I've just run over his cat. Have I missed something? 'I was wondering when you were going to show your face. To be honest, I thought it would be much sooner than this.' I joke referring to the last time he came knocking on my door. He glares at me, clearly not taking to my joke. 'Just like old times.' I laugh.

'You left Gracie to walk on her own last night,' Andy accuses me through gritted teeth. I could've sworn I just saw steam coming out of his ears. How did he find out about that then? Oh. Fuck. She must've told him. Fuck me, it didn't take her long at all to go running back to Mr Perfect then. And I literally had one job.

'Oh please,' I laugh, hiding the feeling of dread in my stomach. 'I bet you came and picked her up,' I tease, trying to fish for answers.

'That's beside the point,' Andy says awkwardly. He did. He picked her up. Shit.

'Mate, she has you wrapped around her little finger,' I mock him, trying to think fast. It can't be too late; I have to fix this.

'Stay away from her,' he warns me. This is all too familiar.

'I mean, I could but we all know that she always comes running back to me,' I wink at him. He's getting angrier if that's even possible. His face is red and I can see his eyes tearing up. I feel sorry for him. I don't know what Gracie is doing to him, but I know it can't be good. He's always been a game to her. I never understood why Gracie did it, but she's really put him through it. 'Mate, she really isn't worth it, look at what she's doing to you.' I say looking down at his clenched fists. For a second, some weak shit comes over for me and I really do feel for him. Gracie drives me crazy and I can only imagine it's worse for him. She used to play him for sport.

'He's a right little mummy's boy, I don't think I have actually seen him do anything for himself,' she laughs. 'Trust me he's a loser.'

'Why are you still with him then?' I ask and her smile vanishes.

'That's my business,' she says bluntly. 'Nothing to do with you and you knew that before we started this.' She dangles that over me every time I ask her a question. I wish I never agreed to it, I deserve at least some of the truth.

'And what do you say to him about me?' I ask teasing, trying to lighten the situation.

'Nothing,' she says, 'you're a secret'. Her words are like bullets.

'Shut up!' Andy shouts.

'You want to be careful,' I warn. 'She is lying to you and you need to stop falling for her shit!' I'm trying to say anything and everything that will keep him away from her. Surely, he can't be that much of an idiot to see the red flags?

'She isn't lying!' He shouts defending her.

'Mate, she's faking this whole thing,' I blurt out before I can stop myself. Maybe if he realises what's going on, he will finally leave her alone.

'No, she's not!' He shouts back.

Louie

'You don't even know the half of it,' I say,
laughing at the irony to that comment. I barely get my
words out when he steps forward and punches me in the
face. What the fuck? I look down at his pathetic little face.
He's got another thing coming if he thinks he can just
march over to my house and punch me in the face.

6

*

After a few hours of trying and failing to contact Gracie, I give up and decide to try and find her in person. She's gone radio silent on me. She's mad, I already know that. But why? Because I was a dick yesterday or because I took her out of the house, just to leave her and let Andy swoop in? Which Gracie is ignoring me? This is all too confusing; I feel like my brain is going to explode. And I can only imagine that sending Andy home with his tail between his legs has only made things worse.

'Oh,' she whispers, looking disappointed when she sees it's me on the other side of the door. This isn't Gracie.

'Hello babe,' I say stepping into the house and pretending that last night didn't happen.

'What are you doing here?' She asks.

'I thought I'd come here and get your apology for leaving last night.'

'For what?' She asks looking confused.

'Just say sorry and then we can move on from this,' I say simply wanting this conversation to be over. Another no show from Gracie, I don't have the patience for this right now.

'No,' she says. Her tone surprises me. I didn't expect her to stick up for herself. I thought she'd back down as usual. Shit. I can't lose her now. Gracie will be so pissed at me.

'Gracie, if you break up with me, then I have no choice but to tell everyone your little secret,' I say smiling. 'There is no point in denying it, we both know what's going on here.' Sadly, it seems the only way I am going to get through this is by threatening her. Again.

'Oh really,' she says, a smile forming on her face. What is she so happy about? It's pissing me off, where have these balls suddenly come from? She's got to be bluffing.

'Yes!' I shout, raising my voice louder than hers. I am not about to let this fool try and walk all over me.

'I think I'll take my chances,' she winks at me. What the fuck? I'm shocked by the way she is acting right now; she's acting so different to before, she is acting like–

'Gracie!' I realise. I have been standing in this room with her for like two minutes, how did I not notice?

'I don't know what you're talking about,' she teases. I smile, realising it's finally her.

'I was wondering when I was going to see you again,' I smile stepping forward and closer to her. 'I've missed you.'

'I don't know what you're talking about,' she repeats, taking a step back. This time her voice is harsh and serious.

'Don't be like this, I did what you said,' I say almost begging and trying to look into her eyes. She avoids my contact at all costs, looking away and not letting me touch her in anyway. The lights from Gracie's dad's car pulling up on the drive catches her attention. 'Gracie.'

'What?' She says looking at me as if I'm the crazy one.

'Where have you been?' I ask. 'What is going on?' All my questions just spill out of me. 'How is there two of you? Who is she?'

'I don't know what you're talking about,' she says again.

'Are you fucking serious?' I shout.

I hear Gracie's dad unlocking the door and turn to see him walking through. He freezes when he sees us both standing there. I'm so angry. I've been jumping through hoops all this week for Gracie to just stand here now and deny it all. Her dad looks at us expectantly, waiting for one of us to say something. Fuck this!

'Are you going to tell him or am I?' I ask looking at Gracie's dad.

'Tell me what?' Her dad says, placing his bag on the floor and slipping his coat off.

'Gracie has been lying to you this whole time,' I say, ignoring her dagger eyes on me. She might be able to make a fool out of Andy, but not me. Her eyes are on me, warning me. I'm too angry to care. 'There is two of them. She has a secret twin.' I blurt out. All the suspicions and theories that have been rushing through my brain and that was my most logical answer. But hearing it out loud, I just sound fucking crazy. My anger is making me stupid.

'Twins?' Gracie's dad looks at me like I've got a massive knob growing off my forehead. 'Good one,' he starts to laugh. He's laughing but this isn't funny, I'm not joking.

'Right,' Gracie says, mocking me with her smile, but her eyes are saying something else. 'Well done, you got me.' She laughs too. They're both laughing **at** me.

'Maybe you should go,' Gracie's dad suggests, although something tells me it's not just a suggestion. 'It's our dinner time and there's not enough food for you.' He looks at me as if I've gone mad, but in his eyes I have. If I had just watched someone have the reaction that I just had then I would think the same. He gives me a sympathetic smile as he walks away and into the kitchen, he feels sorry for me, he thinks that I'm pathetic.

'Gracie, you're making me crazy,' I say quietly embarrassed. My blood is boiling, but I know that I can't just storm out. Who knows when it will be her again? 'Please, just let me in, tell me what's going on here. You know how I feel about you; you know I can help.'

'Louie, you have just showed me that I can't trust you,' she says sadly. I see tears slowly forming in her eyes and I can tell I've hurt her by saying that, but what was I supposed to do? How was I supposed to act in that moment?

'Please, Gracie,' I beg. I am actually begging her. Even after she just made me look like a complete fool. She blinks away her tears and any emotion she was feeling disappears from her face.

'I made it all up,' she says simply.

'Made it up?' I ask, 'Made what up?'

'It's been me all along,' she says.

'Not possible,' I reply. She's lying, I know it. 'I don't believe that.'

'Believe it or not but you said it yourself, you're going crazy,' she smirks, using my own words against me. I'm not going to let her push me away like this, not again.

'Gracie, please.'

'Louie, I was bored, that's all,' she says sounding irritated.

'No. I don't believe that for a second,' I reply. 'All this a game, why did you come back then? To trick me, to mess me around? No, it's bullshit. There's something going on here, I know it.'

'Believe what you want, I don't care.' I've watched her manipulate and lie to other people before, but she can't do it to me, I can see straight through it all.

She can't lie to me and pretend this isn't happening. I can't stand here and listen to her lies anymore. I step forward and pull her face towards mine, kissing her before she can protest. There's no fight in her, instead she falls into me and her hands move to a familiar place on my chest. Her lips follow mine as she pushes her body closer to mine. I move my hands from her face and down her body, holding her tight. Our kisses become more aggressive and with my heart racing so much, I start to lose my breath. I pull away for a moment.

'You do care, I know you do,' I whisper, holding her close to me. 'Let me in. I love you and I know you love me too; I can help you. You don't have to do whatever this is alone. Please.' I say everything I should have said two years ago, maybe if I had, things would be different now. Her tearful eyes are on mine and we're both still for a peaceful few seconds.

'No,' she whispers, reaching up and pulling my hands away from her. She blinks away her tears before they can even fall.

'I can't beg you to love me anymore. I can't keep chasing something that won't let me catch it. Just give me anything, something to hold on to. Please.' I beg. Everything inside me is telling me not to say these things to her, it's making me look weak and vulnerable, but I know what it's like to regret not saying it. I watch as she wipes away one final tear and takes a step away from me. When she looks up, the look she gives me makes me feel sick.

'There's nothing to hold on to,' she says simply. 'I don't love you. Like I said it's all been a game.' Her words sting.

'Fine.' I say feeling the heat in my body rise to my cheeks. 'I'll go. You've fucked with me too much. You're the one who's fucking crazy.' I say feeling the hurt and anger take over. 'You're a selfish bitch. It's easier to hate you than to love you anyway.'

I open the front door and take a step out. I feel a grim feeling in my stomach as my brain starts to make sense of everything. The past few weeks, the past two years and everything before.

'I hate you!'

Those final words haunted me for so long. I don't want to spend the next two years in regret again.

'I know you're lying, but I've done everything I can and I'm done. But if it ever comes to it, I'm here,' I say. The words are hard to say and feel like daggers in my throat, I can't even turn around to look at her. But I just needed to say it. For me to know I have done everything I can. I shut the door behind me before I can say anymore and feel that familiar sharp sting in my heart.

Louie

7

*

A few days later,

an unknown number calls my phone.

It's Gracie,

finally asking for help.

Gracie

Gracie

1

*

I am lying on an old mattress, it's too thin and I can feel the floor underneath it. I try to look around, but it's dark. The light from the window is trying to fight its way in, but there are wooden planks nailed to the wall that's blocking it. Only a thin line of light shines through giving me just enough light to see where I am. I'm in tiny room. The single mattress fills it, leaving only a small space in front of the door. My arm reaches under the mattress and slowly pulls out a knife.

I stand up and walk towards the door, tightly clutching the handle of the knife in my hand and slowly open the door. The hallway is much brighter, my eyes take a second to adjust before I look around. There's nothing here, just two more doors and stairs. An escape. I start to creep down the stairs.

Each step is planned as I slowly descend cringing at every squeak in the floorboard. As I get closer to the bottom, I feel my heart beating faster and the palms of my hands getting sweatier. I'm nervous. Each silent step sends a celebration through my body.

Just. One. More. Step.

The pressure from my foot on the final step releases a scream. My stomach drops and I freeze. I stop and listen.

My ears are searching for something, anything that will indicate my next move. The house is quiet. The anticipation is killing me. My pulse is pounding through my ears and I can feel the blood rushing to my cheeks. I nervously tighten my grip on the knife handle.

The silence tells me to carry on and I lightly take my foot off the final stair. I feel my heart beginning to calm and the terror in my toes starts to vanish. The bottom of the stairs leads me to a living room. The TV is on but there is no one here, I look to my right and see the front door. Quickly I rush over to the door. I hear a loud bang in the back of the house, somethings burning, I can smell it. My shaky fingers struggle to open the locks.

Finally, freedom, I pull down on the door handle and open it.

> *'Boo!'*

A figure stands in front of me, stopping me. Her dark eyes are wild, her black, almost blue hair is crazy. She laughs at me.

> *'I've caught you again,' she says, 'will you ever learn?'*

> *'I have learnt,' I say simply.*

I pull out the knife from behind my back, driving it into her heart and then pulling it free. She falls to the floor.

Gracie

'You can't leave!' She shouts, 'Where are you going to go? They don't want you.' She starts to cough; blood is sputtering out of her mouth.

My eyes shoot open and I am breathless. My mind finally catches up reminding me that it's just a dream, it's all over now. For a second, I relax before bright light suddenly forces itself through my eyeballs. I squint, trying to work out where I am but my vision is blurred. I feel pressure on my arm, squeezing it then releasing and coldness pushing through my veins. I blink to try and focus my eyes when I feel someone's hand on my head, pulling my eyelids open and shining light into them again. I pull my head away and see a woman standing in front of me, pulling off the band on my arm, she smiles at me and wheels away a machine. There are people standing at the end of my bed. I think they're doctors; they look like it, with scrubs and stethoscopes around their necks. I think I'm in a hospital? How did I get here? I want to speak to them, to ask they why I'm here but before I can, they all walk away, leaving me alone.

I stare up at the ceiling, my eyes are finally starting to clear. What happened to me?

'Gracie?' A familiar voice, I turn to see Andy standing at the door. He's leaning against the door frame with his arms crossed. His face is unreadable, what is going on?

'Where am I?' I ask.

'You're in the hospital,' he explains walking into the room. He sits down on a chair next to my bed. He looks so different. 'Gracie, where have you been?' He asks.

'Am I hurt?' I ask too distracted to answer him. I'm in hospital, I must be hurt.

'We don't think so, they're just running some tests to make sure you aren't,' he explains. His answer confuses me, what does that mean? People come to hospitals when they're hurt not when they might be.

'Why do you need to make sure?' I ask.

'You've been missing for two years,' he says sounding like he is stating the obvious. I can tell he's irritated, but he's trying to hide it. 'Where were you?'

Two years? I haven't been missing for two years. It's only been a few days since I last saw him, I'm sure of it. I was at his house, with him. We were in his room and—

I look up at him and really look, studying his face. He's wearing a worried expression and now I can't help but notice how different he looks. He has dark stubble on his chin, since when could he grow facial hair? His face seems thinner and suddenly he has cheek bones. Where did those come from? He looks, well he looks older.

'I don't know,' I say the first thing that comes to mind. I have completely lost all my words. I know what he's saying but I can't understand it. It feels impossible.

'What!' He shouts, I flinch looking up at him in shock. His voice completely pulls me out of my head. Why is he so angry? He is staring at me with worried eyes and it's contagious, I feel myself starting to panic too. What has happened? I stare back, not knowing what else to do or say. He clears his throat and then his face softens, 'Gracie, do you know who I am?'

I do.

'I don't know you.' I say simply. The words just fall out of my mouth so easily.

'Come on, look at me, you know me,' he replies, desperately staring into my eyes.

YES. I KNOW YOU!

'I don't,' I reply bluntly.

'What!' Andy shouts again. His voice echoes through the room as he stands up. His chair falls back, the crash of the metal on the floor makes me flinch but my scream is trapped inside me too.

He looks at me in desperation, his face is red and his eyes are full of tears. Two nurses appear at the door before he can say anything else, they rush into the room towards me. Behind them are two police officers, they strut over to Andy and grab his arms. He tries to fight free but his arms are locked. They pull him out of the room. His voice fights to be heard, I can still hear him shouting from outside the room. One of the nurses checks on me and I tell her I'm

fine, then all of the chaos disappears leaving me
completely alone again.

I pull my blanket off me; heat is rushing through my body
and it's suffocating. I sit up in the bed and try to breath.
The heat rises up my neck and I feel sweat gathering on my
skin. I push myself off the bed and stand up, the cold floor
on my feet is refreshing. I walk towards the window and
pull the drip I'm attached to with me. The wheel drags
along the floor, squeaking quietly.

The sunlight on my skin feels good and helps me start to
feel calm. The sun is slowly setting but the world outside is
showing no sign of stopping. The streetlights slowly start
to replace the sun. I try to focus my thoughts to work out
what's happening. Two years? Could it really have been
that long?

Where did I go? When did I come back? How? I should be
freaking out, the thought of it alone is scary but I still don't
believe it. This doesn't happen. The light outside starts to
dim and as it gets darker outside, the bright, artificial light
from inside takes over. It slowly starts to reveal my
reflection on the window. I stare at myself as I appear in
the window. At first, it's just an outline, then my features
start to form. My nose, my eyes, my mouth. It can't have
been two years; I look exactly the same. Andy must be
wrong; he could be confused or maybe he's joking. This
could all be one big joke. Then I see it. My hair. My
shoulder length hair, it's almost down to my hip. My
stomach sinks and I feel bile rise in the back of my throat.

Gracie

Chills cover my body as the realisation starts to hit. My pulse start to going crazy underneath my skin an—

'Gracie,' a small voice says my name, distracting and saving me from my panic. I turn around to see Penny standing at the door, in the exact same place Andy was before.

'You scared me,' I say simply, pointing out my surprise.

'What were you doing?' She asks accusingly.

'Nothing.' I say with a straight face. She looks unconvinced and without any welcome she walks into the room. Her eyes are still stalking mine when she sits down on the chair that Andy had slammed into the floor. She sits in silence watching me as I slowly walk back to the bed.

'I'm sorry about Andy, he's taking this quite hard,' she explains. Her voice is patronising and undermining towards Andy and his feelings. I hate that.

'That's ok,' I say simply, desperate for her to change the subject.

'Do you know who I am?' She asks.

'No,' I say.

'Okay, well,' she pauses for a second, tilting her head. 'I'm Penny, I'm your dad's **best** friend,' she says, emphasising her title and very clearly marking her territory.

'My dad?' It didn't occur to me until now, why is she here instead of my parents? 'Where is he?'

'He's been working away recently, but he's trying to get back as soon as possible,' she explains. I feel a sting when I go to ask about my mum and before I can say anything, Penny changes the subject. 'Where have you been Gracie?'

'I don't know,' I admit.

'And you have no memory of your life before you went missing?' Her questions are so blunt. I can tell she's not convinced by my answers.

'Nope,' I shake my head. She nods, reluctantly accepting my answer. My last words linger as silence fills the room, it feels heavy and uncomfortable.

'Right, well I'll leave you to be on your own for a while,' she says standing up. I feel relieved as she speaks, like I can finally breath again. 'I'm going to head out and buy you some things that you'll need. I'm sure that will be the last thing on your dad's mind when he gets here.'

'Ok.' I say simply.

I watch as she backs out of the room, her eyes still glued to mine. She stands at the door for a few seconds, in painful silence. Why is she staring at me like that?

'Thank you,' I say, wondering if that's what she was waiting for. She gives me a forced smile before finally leaving me alone.

Gracie

Andy's laugh erupts, sending echoes through the house as I walk into the living room. I try to hide my smile, after all he's laughing at me. My dad is trying to hide his amusement, but I can just tell he's laughing inside too.

'Guys, stop!' I warn, feeling embarrassed. I look down at the dress knowing that they're right, it's hideous. 'This the is the last time I am ever going to ask for your opinion.'

'Oh no, we don't mean to laugh do we Andy?' My dad asks looking over at him, then they both erupt into more laughter. I hate that, it's like they can read each other's mind.

'It's just that,' Andy pauses, clearly choosing his next words very carefully. 'Oh baby, it's awful, you can't wear that.'

'That bad?' I ask, already knowing the answer. The frills on the dress are in a very unfortunate place and the burgundy satin is unforgiving.

'Yes,' my dad replies before anyone else can answer. All three of us burst into laughter. It really is bad. I hear my mum's voice, calling my dad into the kitchen. He responds, leaving Andy and me standing in the living room alone.

'I know you want me to tell you that you look beautiful and you do, but I really don't think I will be able leave the house with you wearing that, let alone prom pictures,' he teases.

'It looked different in the picture online,' I defend myself. He laughs wrapping his arms around me.

'I hate to say it, but I think you've been scammed,' he replies, I nod in agreement as he leans in to kiss me. 'Now, why don't you let me help you take this monstrosity off,' he whispers into my ear.

'Gracie,' I look up immediately and see my dad standing at the door. He is leaning on the door frame with his arms crossed. I wonder how long he's been standing there; I was completely distracted in my own head.

It's daylight again, I didn't even notice. Time seems to be passing so quickly, it doesn't even feel like that long since Penny left and that was yesterday.

'Hi,' I reply to him quietly. My head starts to feel heavy and I desperately try to hold back the tears that have suddenly rushed towards the back of my eyes.

His face lights up and he walks straight towards me. I flinch as he gets too close, I think if I let him hug me, even touch me at all then I'd lose it. He notices before getting too close and slowly backs away and sits down on the chair everyone else has been sitting on. His smile is piercing through me, I can tell he is trying to reassure me with it, but it's not working.

He hasn't changed that much and when I look at him, it feels like no time has passed. I needed some familiarity especially from him. He is the same, even the way his hair is parted. But then I notice the grey hairs, the slightly wrinkled eyes and dull skin making the two years more noticeable. That sinking feeling in my stomach returns.

'Do you know who I am?' He asks slowly. I can see it in his eyes, the hope that I will say yes and I want to say yes so badly. It's one word, one simple word that I know he'd give anything to hear.

'No' I say quickly.

'Gracie, I'm your dad.' He says tearfully.

'Penny told me you were coming,' I explain, needing to say something to fill the silence.

He nods and for a few seconds he just sits there staring at me and the silence returns making me feel uncomfortable.

'So, where is my mum?' I ask quickly, before I can chicken out. I don't know how, but I think already know. I just need it confirmed, I need to hear it from him.

'Your mum?' He repeats slowly. I nod. His reaction if enough of a confirmation already. 'Gracie, your mum is no longer with us, she died not long after you went missing.'

'She's gone?' I whisper, saying it aloud for what feels like the first time.

'She died.' He repeats, his words sting more than they did the first time. 'I know this might be hard for you, even if you can't remember but—' I zone out, his words drown out and my pulse takes over my ears.

'I need a minute,' I manage to put the words together.

'Uh, yes,' he says standing up abruptly, 'of course'.

I hold my breath until he's gone, too scared to show any emotion in front of him. I don't know how I am supposed to react to this. How did I even know? When did I find out? I don't remember it, but I've felt this before. It's familiar but that doesn't mean it hurts any less. There's so much, guilt, sadness, grief and anger, I don't know what to feel first. I close my eyes in attempt to block it out. Anxiety is rising up my throat.

I start to let myself fall further and further away from reality to that familiar, safe place. The further I go, the less I feel. It numbs me. So, I carry on going to that dark place in my thoughts where I can't feel anything.

When I wake up the next morning, it takes me a second to realise that I'm no longer in the hospital. I sit up and look around, this room feels familiar. I think I'm in Penny's spare room. The last thing I remember is my dad walking out of my room in the hospital and now I'm here at Penny's. I pull the covers off me and stand up, my legs feel wobbly. I walk towards the mirror on the wall and stare at myself focusing on my eyes. The familiarity calms me.

I look away and towards the door when I hear something outside it. I quickly grab the door handle and pull it towards me. I flinch when I see Andy standing there, he's standing so close. He jumps back when he sees me, seemingly more surprised to see me than I am to see him. Did he not know I was here? I didn't even know I was here. A smile spreads across his face as his leans back on the wall behind him.

'Oh, uh. Hi Gracie,' he says scratching his head, 'I was just checking if you were awake.'

'I'm awake,' I say simply.

'I was going to make some breakfast, I wanted to know if you wanted some?' He offers, staring at the floor. It's awkward and he's acting so strange, maybe because I haven't seen him since he stormed out of my hospital room.

'Uh yea.' I say trying to ignore how uncomfortable it is between us, 'let me get ready and I'll meet you downstairs.' I suggest, looking up and waiting for a response. After a few painful seconds of silence, I give up on a response and turn around and back into the room.

'Uh Gracie,' he mumbles. I barely hear him, but I feel his hand reaching out to mine. I turn around to look at him. 'Do you remember?' He asks, his eyes are glued to the floor.

216

'No Andy,' I say simply.

'You really don't remember us?' He asks, his voice louder this time and finally he's looking up at me. He sounds so hurt.

'No,' I reply, suddenly feeling guilt rising inside me.

'Me and you?' He steps towards me, getting even closer. He's not even touching me, but I can feel the heat radiating off his skin onto mine. I struggle to find the words to answer him, everything in my brain has gone to mush. He lingers there for a few more seconds and without permission my eyes shoot towards his lips. My brain is flooded with memories of kissing him. My eyes lose focus as he gets even closer. The urge to kiss him becomes impossible to ignore.

Before I can think it through, I lean forward and kiss him. Our lips touch but he doesn't react, he doesn't move. I quickly pull away in reaction to his rejection but before I can feel any embarrassment, I feel his hands reach up to my face. He pulls me back and kisses me. My thoughts start to race, arguing with me to stop. It feels too good to stop. I need to stop.

I reach up and wrap my arms around his neck. Every thought in my head telling me to stop vanishes when I feel his body press against mine and his hands down my back. Thoughts of his hands, where they are and where they are going overpower anything else in my brain. I can feel his heart beating against my chest. The smell, the taste, the feeling of his warm kisses is so familiar, so comforting.

My brain finally catches up, forcing me to stop.

'I'm sorry,' I say breathlessly and push Andy's shoulders gently away from me. He looks up at me, his face is red and he's out of breath too. Disappointment washes over his face, but he quickly hides it.

'It's ok,' he says softly. I look up at him, at his lips, feeling withdrawal from him already.

'It just felt right,' I try to explain.

'You really don't need to be sorry,' he says simply. 'I'll see you downstairs.'

I walk back into the room and shut the door behind me. I stand back in front of the mirror and stare at myself. My lips are swollen and my cheeks are red, I stare at the skin on my neck and lightly touch where his lips were.

Why am I lying to him? To everyone? I do remember, I have the whole time. So why did I tell them I couldn't? Why am I only realising this now? I need to tell him the truth.

When I get downstairs, I am going to tell him.

2

*

As I walk down the stairs, I stare at the pictures on the wall. All inspirational quotes; *live, life, love.* Eugh! Yep, I am definitely at Penny's house. Back to square one, great! The house is completely silent. Maybe there's no one here and I'm alone. Oh god, I hope so. Although, I'm sure they wouldn't leave poor, pathetic Gracie all by herself though. As I reach the bottom of the stairs, my question is unfortunately answered when Andy appears in front of me. He's looking up at me with the biggest, cheesiest smile on his face. What's his deal? Why is he just standing there staring at me? I look down at him and force a smile. He hasn't changed a bit in the past two years, well a little bit of facial hair, more like bum fluff, but at least now he can finally shave, bless.

'You look nice,' he says, the sickening grin on his face is only getting bigger. I look down at my clothes, it's just a jumper and some black legging. It's hardly anything worth a compliment. What a fucking wet wipe.

'Thanks,' I reply stopping at the bottom of the stairs. He looks down at me, still smiling like a fucking psycho. He ought to be careful, if the wind changes, he'll be stuck looking like an absolute mong.

'Mum and Connor have gone shopping,' he explains walking into the kitchen, I follow him looking around the room. The walls are full of photographs, ones of Gracie and Andy when they were younger, Connor and Penny at school together and even more of Andy's chubby face.

'Orange juice? Tea?' Andy asks pulling my attention away from the wall.

'I don't like orange juice, but I'll have a tea.' I say sitting down on a stool in front of the breakfast bar. I see a laptop sitting on the side, open for anyone to take. I wonder if Andy will leave me alone for long enough for me to use it. I need to find out about Jane.

'Two sugars,' we say together. The words are already out of my mouth before I can stop them. I cringe and Andy looks over to me and smiles. He laughs to himself and the urge to roll my eyes is hard to ignore, but I control it.

'I must have made you hundreds of cups of tea,' he continues, his smile beaming.

'Hundreds, wow!' I say knowing sarcasm will be the only way to get through this conversation without blowing my cover.

'We were in a relationship for nearly three years, that adds up to a lot of tea,' he explains in his best children's presenter voice. He walks around the breakfast bar and closer to me. I consider running but his strides are big and no match for my small legs and the fact I'm sat down. Ugh, please don't. He stops in front of me and takes one of my hands in his. I don't want to look up, I can feel him staring down into my soul and this time I'm fighting the urge to projectile vomit. I psyche myself up and finally look up at him. He's gazing down at me in a very sickening way. I am Gracie, I remind myself. It's too early to blow my cover. So, I count down the seconds, wondering when he is going to look away. He's held my eye contact for way too long, he must nearly be finished with his creepy staring. Oh no. He's getting closer. As if he's going to kiss me. Oh. Wait. I look at his scrawny lips puckering up. He is going to kiss me. No. No. No. No. My brain goes into survival mode and I clear my throat loudly, interrupting his moment. It works and he quickly backs away from me.

What the hell was that? Why on earth does he think he can come over here and try to kiss me? Clearly Gracie has given him some sort of green light there. Can that dumb bitch not keep her legs closed for two seconds?

'So, what do you want?' He asks, finally at a reasonable but not desirable distance away from me. No distance is too far in my opinion. 'For breakfast I mean,' he adds quickly.

'I'll have a dippy egg,' I say thinking of something that's quick. I don't want to sit in here with him for any longer than I have to. Cereal would be a better choice, but I know he'd insist on cooking something. He looks up, seemingly amused by my request. I don't get it. What's so funny about that?

Gracie

'Dippy eggs?' He repeats. I answer his question with a glare, before remembering who I'm supposed to be. 'Dippy eggs it is then,' he says turning to the kettle and switching it on.

Whatever this is that's going on between Andy and Gracie, it needs to stop. Now. Gracie trusts him too much; if he finds out the truth it will ruin everything. Plus, I don't want his germs anywhere near my mouth. It's vital they think she lost her memory; it will be the only way I can be fully in control without getting caught out. I just can't believe Gracie fell for it so easily, she didn't even question it, what a dumb bitch.

We need to stay here long enough for us to be able to leave without being *'missing'*, so I can finally be free. I take another glance at the laptop and wonder how risky it would be if I asked to use it, maybe I should wait until I'm more settled.

3

*

'Andy, I have to tell you something,' I say as I walk into Penny's kitchen. He is standing by the oven, facing the wall. He turns around and smiles at me.

'I love you; you can tell me anything,' he says walking towards me. His smile is encouraging.

'Andy, look,' I hesitate for a second.

'Come on,' he says playfully, taking my hands in his.

'Andy, I haven't lost my memory, I remember you, I remember everything,' I announce.

'What?' Andy says, he loosens his grip on my hands and drops them. 'You lied?'

'I didn't lie, I mean, I did, but I didn't realise that I was lying,' I try to explain.

'You're a liar,' his eyebrows scrunch up in anger.

'You lied?' I turn around to see my dad standing there, his face is full of sadness and disappointment.

'No, I didn't, I mean I did but it's not what you think,' I struggle to find any more words and when I open my mouth, nothing comes out.

223

'Of course, she lied,' Penny appears in front of me. 'Gracie, is an entitled, spoilt little bitch, she loves to play us all like a game,' Penny bursts out into laughter.

My dad's face lifts in amusement then him and Andy start to laugh too. Their laughter erupts over me, it surrounds and suffocates me.

'Gracie!' I turn to see my mum standing at the door. 'Do we not deserve the truth?'

'You're heartless,' Andy shouts.

'We were better off without your lies,' my dad shouts.

'Go back to that dark place, Gracie,' Penny laughs.

Her final words hit me before they all disappear, leaving me completely alone, in darkness.

I open my eyes and light surrounds me. I quickly sit up and grab my bed frame to steady myself. I'm hot, sweat is covering my whole body. I pull the covers off my body and cold air attacks it. I finally catch my breath and start to feel my heart begin to calm. It takes me a second to realise I am in my bed, in my old room.

Everything is the same, but it feels different. I thought it would just feel normal, like when you come back from a long holiday, it's not. I stand up and walk around the room. It's as if nothing has been touched in that last two years, everything is exactly where I left it. Before everything disappeared.

I look up at the wall at the photos I stuck there when I was 15. There's so many, with Andy, with some of the girls from school; I wonder where they are now and my mum. I stare at a photo of her and me at the beach, looking at it stings. Her smile was so beautiful, I almost never saw her without it. She stares back at me and guilt suffocates me. How could I lie about forgetting her? How could anyone possibly forgive that? I turn away from the wall, I can't look at it anymore.

I need to get out of this room. I see my dressing gown hanging on the back of my door and slip it on. It's half ten in the morning, I must've been asleep for hours, although I don't remember going to bed or much of yesterday either. It feels like I have been awake all night and the bags under my eyes look like they are feeling the same way.

As I walk into the kitchen, I see Andy sat at the kitchen table. His phone is lit up in his hands, but his eyes are focused in front of him, he's completely out of it. I wanted to tell him the truth, but after that dream, I don't think it's such a good idea. It may have been a dream, but I didn't have it for no reason, it must be a sign or something. He's hurt as it is, imagine if he found out I was lying too.

'Andy,' I say trying to get his attention.

Gracie

'Gracie, you're awake,' he says snapping out of it. He looks up and a smile spreads across his face. He places his phone down on the table.

'And you're here,' I say surprised but happy to see him. I was worried he was going to be distant with me. I haven't seen him since our kiss yesterday.

'I took a few days off work, so we could spend some time together,' he explains.

'Good,' I say slowly wondering what that means. Then I realise, he has a job. Well, of course he has a job, but I didn't even think about that, about him having a job. A job where? Doing what? This is everything I have missed out on.

I walk over to the fridge and open it. Maybe I could just ask him casually, like I'm making conversation or something? I reach into the fridge and pull out a carton of orange juice. I mean he mentioned work first, it wouldn't look too weird if I asked about it. I look around the kitchen and wonder if the glasses are still in the same place.

'I thought you didn't like orange juice,' he points out standing up. He walks closer and stops right in front of me. He reaches out behind me and opens one of the kitchen cupboards. I blush as he gets closer and I try not to think about the familiar smell of his skin. He hands me a small glass with a smile.

'I never said that,' I say coming back to reality, where did he get that from?

'Right,' he says slowly looking just as confused as me, 'tea?'

'Yea, sure,' I reply pouring the juice into the glass he gave me. I watch as he fills the kettle with water and turns it on. I sit down at the kitchen table and take a sip of my juice. I can't help but wonder what has happened in the past two years? Things must've changed for him, I mean he has a job, there's probably more I don't know. I wonder why he didn't go to university, we used to talk about it a lot. Is there someone else in his life? He hasn't mentioned anyone, but he hasn't not mentioned anyone either. Maybe that's why I didn't see him after our kiss, he needed to get away from me. Surely not? He can't be with someone else, there's no way. But then, for him it's been two years, even if that's nothing to me. I look up and see Andy staring at me.

'Why are you looking at me like that?' I ask, logically pushing the thought that he's reading my mind away.

'No reason,' he says vaguely, turning around as the kettle clicks. Maybe now is the time I can casually ask him about his life without giving anything away, just a casual conversation about where he works. I can do that, that's normal. I'll just—

The doorbell interrupts my questions before I can even ask them.

'I can get it,' Andy says.

Gracie

'No, I'll get it, this is my house,' I say playfully. I stand up and walk out the kitchen. When I turn my head, I see Andy is close behind me. I speed up to get there first and he starts to laugh when my socks slip on the floor. I grab the door handle before he can, laughing and open the door.

Oh. No.

I feel my face fall. My stomach has just fallen out of me and is now just chilling by my feet. Standing in front of me, with his dark hair and brown eyes and of course he's wearing that stupid leather jacket and that mischievous smile. Some things never change.

'Hello trouble,' I feel my cheeks heat up.

'Louie,' Andy says before I can speak. I actually did forget about him. Not that there was much to remember, but a tiny indiscretion in a time of loneliness, which he never let me forget. It was barely anything, that's why I'm surprised he's standing here right now. 'She doesn't know who you are Louie, she doesn't remember,' Andy adds.

'Surely Gracie can speak for herself,' he says winking at me, I melt, but not in the good way. Normally I would agree with him there, but I'd rather not speak to him. I look back to Andy, his eyes are on Louie and if it was possible, there would be smoke coming out of his eyes and ears. The tension between them two of them is toxic, it always has been.

'Do you remember me?' Louie asks, his eyes are heavy on mine.

'No,' I say quietly, trying to avoid his eye contact. He's grinning, he seems amused by all of this and it's making me feel very nervous.

'It's been a while, I'd love a catch up,' he says, raising his eyebrows and gesturing for me to step outside with him.

'I, uh.'

'You'd think a person who lost their memory would do everything they could to find out about their old life and I was part of that life,' Louie says before I can answer.

He was barely part of my life, but I can't say that and he knows it. I don't understand why he's here and what he's gaining from it. But he's right. I would want to find out as much as I could about my old life.

'Gracie, you don't have to listen to him,' Andy warns, but I ignore him. I want to know what he wants; Louie wouldn't just drop by for no reason. I can tell he knows something, but I don't know how that would be possible. Still, I'm not taking any chances, for now I need to keep this secret to myself. 'Gracie if you could just remember, you would know he is bad news!' Andy shouts. I know that Louie is bad news. I also know that this is already a very complicated situation and involving Louie is only going to make it worse. I slowly take a step out of the house and shut the door behind me. Louie is already sat down on the bench outside my house.

'I can't believe your back,' he says as I sit down, 'I've been wanting to come and see you ever since I heard.' His words catch me off guard, he looks serious and he actually seems genuine. It's weird. 'Where did you go?'

'I don't know, I don't remember,' I say simply. He nods slowly as I speak. Then a weird smile spreads across his face, making me suddenly feel very uncomfortable. The way he is looking at me weird, he's acting like he knows something I don't.

'I don't have much time,' he explains, 'but I would really like to talk to you some more, can I take you to lunch tomorrow?' he asks.

'I'm not really sure what I'm doing tomorrow,' I say awkwardly.

'Great, I'll come by at 12 to pick you up,' he smirks and before I can say anything, he stands up and walks away. I want to shout to him no, but something inside me stops me.

When Louie disappears out of sight, I put my head in my hands and sigh. I need a minute to think about how I am going to tell Andy, he's not going to happy about this. He seems to think a lot more went on with Louie than it actually did.

After a few minutes I stand up and walk back into the house. When I open the door, Andy is sitting on the stairs waiting for me.

'What did he want?' He asks bluntly.

'Lunch, tomorrow,' I say quietly. I can already see from the reaction on his face that he is going to lose it. I don't blame him. Louie antagonised Andy for so long about my little indiscretion.

'You're not going to go, are you?' He almost spits at me.

'He didn't leave me much choice,' I say quietly, walking back into the kitchen and away from the confrontation. I feel bad, I know how much this will hurt him, but I couldn't say no. Louie was right, I would want to know everything and I have to know what he wants. I need to do everything I can to keep this a secret.

The front door slams, shaking the whole house.

'Andy?' I say walking out into the hallway. He's gone.

4

*

Gracie's phone vibrates on my mattress, rudely waking me up. I stretch my arms out and groan loudly. I grab the phone and squint as the screen lights up. Eugh, it's so early. My eyes finally focus to see three missed calls and a message all from Andy. What is that idiot doing trying to call me this early? I click on the message.

> Andy: Gracie, if you go with Louie today, I'm done. I know you don't remember, but I'm not going through this with you and him again.

Louie? Interesting. I really didn't think he would have made an appearance, especially after how we left things. I would've thought he would never want to see me again; at least that's what he said. After that *'dream'* Gracie had the other night, I know she won't be telling anyone the truth anytime soon. The dumb bitch is afraid of her own shadow, bless her. Now all I need to do is keep Andy away and maybe Louie could be just the thing I need to do that. If Gracie gets too close to Andy, then it's all over. I know what they're like, she'll end up telling him everything. Then it will only be a matter of time until they find out about me. To them, I am a parasite, rotting Gracie's precious and innocent little brain. That can't happen, then it will be over and all of this, including the past two years, would be for nothing. I can use Louie to help with my little problem, it's the perfect way to keep Andy away.

But that's it. I think about the last time I saw Louie and what happened. I wonder how he's going to act around me, how I should act. All the memories of him come back, in fact I'm not sure they ever really left, I've just spent too long pushing them away. I can't let myself get distracted with him. I can feel all I want when I'm finally free.

I take one last look at Andy's message and laugh. Bless him, at least he's finally starting to stick up for himself instead of letting us walk all over him again, good for him. I slide the message across the screen and delete it. A second thought crosses my mind. I pull up Andy's contact on Gracie's phone and block him, before making a new contact for him with a random number. Try speaking to him now Gracie. I roll over in the bed and close my eyes. She makes this too easy.

Louie came to the house and collected me at 12 and we ended up in a local café. It's small, with only a few tables and chairs dotted around with some more outside. It's too cold to sit outside so I sit down on a table by the window while Louie orders us some drinks. This place is cute. I look around, the walls are full of old photos of the town throughout history. Each table has a different kind of flower on it and none of the teacups match. It feels familiar, I think Gracie has been here before.

I watch Louie as he stands at the counter, he's speaking to one of the waitresses. I haven't really said much to him since he picked me up. He kept the conversation light and didn't ask me many questions, which is refreshing from how everyone else has been acting with me. They both suddenly turn to look at me, they're clearly talking about me, so I stare back. The waitress starts to look uncomfortable by my death stare and looks away. Louie's amused eyes meet mine and he laughs to himself. I feel butterflies start in my stomach and immediately squash them.

'A vanilla latte for you,' he says putting the drink down and sitting down on the chair opposite me. He smiles as he sits down and I quickly move my attention over to the coffee. He starts to assemble his tea, pouring it and adding milk and sugar. I watch in silence, refusing to say the first words to him. He's being nice but I'm still not 100% where we stand right now.

'You seem different today,' he says, the amusement returning to his face. I can't help but notice how kind these two years have been to him. He was good looking before but now, he's even better. He didn't have that jawline before and he's definitely bulked up. I was kind of hoping he'd gotten ugly; it would make this whole thing a lot easier for me.

The Way Back

'I feel different,' I say simply. Gracie very much hates Louie, so I can only imagine the conversation they had yesterday. I have no idea how he managed to get her to agree to lunch. Although, part of me thinks that Gracie has a little soft spot for him, I know I wasn't fully responsible for the breakdown of Andy and Gracie's relationship two years ago.

'I was sorry to hear about your mum,' he says quietly. I look up and I can tell by the look on his face that he's being genuine. I didn't know about Gracie's mum; although it didn't take me long after moving back into Gracie's house to find out though.

'Thanks,' I reply quickly not wanting to talk about it. As much as I hate Gracie, it's sad, for both of us. An awkward silence rises between us and suddenly no word feels like the right thing to say.

'So, crazy stuff you coming back after all this time, we thought you were a goner,' Louie says, quickly changing the subject. Of course he says something cocky and arrogant but I'm grateful for the distraction.

'Insane,' I reply suddenly feeling lighter. I hold his eye contact for a few seconds and feel those butterflies again.

'You know before you went missing, you and I used to spend a lot of time with each other.' He's teasing me. I know he doesn't believe any of this, I can tell.

'Oh really,' I reply.

'Yes I remember you were always playing games, getting caught up in little lies.' He laughs, 'you weren't the perfect little angel that Andy thought you were, that everyone thought you were.'

'Louie, just say what you want to say, I'm not playing this game,' I say bluntly. The mention of Andy and Gracie dissolves the excitement in our little game. I don't want to play anymore.

'Ha ha, ok,' he says, his eyes lighting up. He knows that he's caught me out. His expression softens. 'You finally got out then?' He asks. 'I knew you would, I just didn't think you'd come back so soon.'

'I ran into some complications,' I admit thinking about the last two years and how wrong everything went.

'Care to expand on that?' He asks.

I ran away, bumped into a mad woman called Jane who manipulated Gracie into trusting her and then trapped us in her house. Telling him would be nice, I trust him but the less he knows, the less anyone knows, the better.

'Not really,' I say quietly.

'Well, it's good to see you. I missed you.' He missed me?

'Please, Gracie,' Louie says, his eyes full of tears. 'I'm asking you to stay.' I look down at him. He is literally

on his knees, begging me to stay and it's taking everything in me not to, but I can't.

'You know that I can't,' I say quietly. He knew this, so why is he now making it so hard for me now? He stands up and grabs my hands, holding them tight.

'Why not?' He begs, the way he's looking at me hurts. I can see the pain in his eyes.

'I can't be myself here,' I explain, feeling tears form in the back of my eyes. I hold them back; I can't let him see me cry.

'Why do you keep saying that? I don't understand, tell me please.' He reaches up, holding my face in his hands. 'Please,' he whispers.

'If you really love me, like you say you do, then you need to let me go,' I say, pulling away from him and turning my face away from him before the tears fall.

'But—'

'And you need to keep it to yourself,' I say cutting him off.

Those cold words still send a shiver down my spine. I look up and see his face fall and I wonder if he was thinking about the same thing. I have the urge to reach out to him but stop when the waitress who served Louie earlier comes over. She places a bowl of chips in front of us and at the same time brings Louie back to reality. He quickly recovers from whatever what going on in his brain and thanks her. And then she continues to just stand there and stare at me. Her face is familiar, but I don't know her. She's just standing there like a moron. It's if she's waiting for me to say something to her.

'Take a picture, it will last longer,' I snap. She jumps up and away from the table. Nosey bitch. I am sick of people staring at me. It's so annoying. I look over at Louie, he's trying to hide his laughter by putting food into his mouth.

'So,' Louie says moving around the food in his mouth, 'it was weird seeing you yesterday, you didn't seem like yourself at all, it—'

'It wasn't me,' I interrupt him, getting straight to the point. I'm not sure how long I can sit here with him, I just need to get what I came here for. He looks up at me, confusion spreading all over his face.

'What?' He stares at me. 'You're saying it wasn't you?' He says slowly, repeating my words back to me.

'I'm saying, it wasn't the Gracie you thought,' I correct.

'Did I speak to you yesterday?' He asks.

'Technically, no,' I explain giving him a cheeky smile.

'What? Like there is two of you?'

'Something like that,' I say, putting a chip into my mouth. He sits in silence and I can almost see the cogs in his brain working overtime to understand.

'Have we met before?' He asks.

'Yes, of course, like you said, we've had some pretty good times,' I explain, feeling a smile grow on my face and immediately try to stop the feeling from spreading. The memories I have been pushing away rush back, along with the feelings that have been lingering inside me, that I've been trying so hard to ignore. Sitting here with him suddenly hurts.

I feel him take my hand. 'Gracie, no more jokes. Please tell me what's going on.' He stares into my soul. This was a mistake. I know Gracie didn't know any better, but this was a bad idea. This is what made leaving the first time so hard.

'I've got to dash,' I say quickly, all of a sudden feeling the need to leave. I stand up and pull my coat off the back of my chair, 'see you later.'

I rush out of the door and into the fresh air. This was a mistake; I should never have involved him. How could I be so stupid? This is what made it so hard the first time, why did I think it was going to be any different?

'Wait!' He shouts, following me out of the café. I stop and turn around. He walks closer to me and I take a step back. He stops, keeping his distance from me. 'Do you need help again?' His eyebrows are scrunched up, he looks worried. I feel my heart warm and immediately punish myself for it. He stares at me waiting for an answer. I sigh, knowing I can trust him. He proved that to me two years ago when he kept all my secrets, even after I left.

And I hate to admit it, but Gracie has become a lot stronger than I thought she would. She has already started to question her memory loss, there's only a matter of time until my manipulation will wear off, the bad dreams won't last forever. I can only control her for as long as she will let me. I know that Louie could help, I just need to keep my distance.

He stares at me, waiting for me to say something. I choose my words carefully, giving him a way to help, without giving him the whole truth.

'Gracie's a catch, you should get her back, keep her safe and away from Andy,' I say slowly.

5

*

When the doorbell rings, I jump up to answer it immediately. I feel like I have been waiting all day to hear it, or at least to hear my phone ring. Andy hasn't said a word to me since he stormed out the other morning, each time I try to get into contact with him. Nothing.

When I open the door and see Louie standing there, I don't even bother to hide my disappointment. He's probably here to collect on the lunch I never went to. I don't have the energy to deal with him right now, so before he can say anything, I push the door shut.

'That's not very polite,' he says putting his foot in the door.

'I have no interest in speaking to you,' I reply simply. Louie can talk his way into anything, so I am not going to give him the chance.

'Well, what have I done to receive this welcome?' He asks, smirking. I am not going to react, I'm not going to let him in this time. 'Surely nothing that you can remember.' I freeze. What does he mean by that? I try to play it cool.

'Why are you here?' I ask, giving in. I know Louie isn't the type of person to just drop by and say hello. He wants something.

'I want a chance with you, again,' he says with confidence. His response surprises me, it was the last thing I was expecting him to say.

'I'm not interested,' I say politely hoping that's enough to make him go away. For a moment I think it is, but then he smirks at me.

'Gracie, I know the truth about everything,' he says.

'You're bluffing,' I reply, there is no way. How could he possibly know anything? I barely know what's going on and it's all in my head.

'Do you really want to test that theory?' He asks raising his eyebrows. I don't know how to respond to him, what to say without giving anything up. 'This isn't really about memory loss, is it?' His bluff is way too close to the truth.

'What do you want?' I ask giving up.

'I want another chance!' He says simply, 'with you, without Andy getting in the way.' A chance? Why would he want another chance with me? The first one wasn't that great in the first place. I don't even know how Louie and I first started seeing each other, but it was brief and not anything special.

'Andy isn't in the way anymore anyway,' I admit. I know what he's like and there has to be another reason he's lurking around, but I don't have the luxury to turn him down. The truth can't come out now, it's too late.

'Perfect!' He smiles and I feel a shiver down my spine. 'So…' I wonder if there is any way out of this.

'Would you like to come in?' I say sighing and rolling my eyes. Any hope I had of Andy coming back is now gone.

'I'd love to!' He says bordering sarcasm. He walks past me, stopping briefly to look at me. I freeze and stare at the floor, not knowing what to do. He reaches out and touches my face, lifting my chin up so I have no choice but to look at him. It feels like he's staring into my soul and I hold my breath. What is he doing? And then he just drops my face without any warning and walks through into the house, kicking his shoes off and making himself comfortable.

It took Louie only a few days to make himself right at home. For someone who had barely been in my house, he seemed to fit in like an old piece of furniture, weirdly knowing where everything is. I walk into the living room to see him sprawled out on the sofa, staring at the TV, eating a share bag of crisps to himself.

'Gracie,' he moans as I walk in.

'Yes,' I say, trying so hard to be nice to him. After all, he has the power to ruin me within seconds, which he has had no issue in reminding me every second I don't agree with him. He's clearly enjoying this a lot and I still can't work out why he is doing it. I just know, it's too late for the truth to come out. And for now, I am doing anything I can to keep my head above the water. That includes playing along in Louie's little games.

'You're letting the light in, shut the door,' he points out, bluntly. I take a breath and try my best to keep all the thoughts I'm having inside my head. I calmly walk back to the door and gently shut it. When I turn back around, Louie is sat up and staring at me. His eyes are focused and are squinting at my face. I stare back, waiting for him to say something.

'What?' He spits at me accusingly.

'Nothing,' I say shrugging my shoulders, ever since he came back, he's been doing that, just staring at me and it's weird.

'We're going to the pub tonight,' he announces, shoving a handful of crisps into his mouth.

'Erm.'

'We're going to the pub tonight,' he repeats with his mouth full, spitting bits of crisp all over the place, I can't help but stare at him in disgust. 'You don't want me to tell everyone your little secret, do you?'

'I didn't say no,' I reply quickly. He is making me miserable.

6

*

I stand in front of the mirror looking at my face. Gracie actually did a good job today on the makeup front, half the time she has no idea what's she's doing but today it's ok. Definitely much better than the other day when she put in me those awful pair of jeans. Fucking mom jeans, who does she think she is?

I poke my head through the living room door and see Louie lying on the sofa. He doesn't notice me standing there. His eyes are glued to something on the other side of the room, his head is somewhere else. That's probably a good thing, I've been trying to keep my distance. I see SpongeBob playing on the TV and laugh to myself, he's definitely not as hard as he makes himself out to be. For a second, the idea of going in there and sitting with him crosses my mind. I know he's waiting for me to make an appearance, but I know it's not a good idea. I can feel when I'm free. It can't be complicated this time, it's too hard. I don't think I'd be able to do it a second time.

'You can go,' I say simply.

'I can go, oh thank you so much oh great one! Are you fucking kidding me Gracie?' Louie shouts. I jump

slightly but I don't let him see that his voice has startled me.

'Fine then,' I shout, matching his tone. 'I'll go,' I stand up dramatically and walk towards my bedroom door. I reach out to grab the door handle and Louie appears in front of me, blocking the door.

'There's no way in hell I am letting you walk out now.' He shouts.

'The conversation is over, there is nothing left to say,' I say simply.

'No, you've finished speaking. It's my turn now,' I look up at him in shock. No one has ever spoken to me like that before. It's so forceful. I bite my lip in order to hide the smile that's desperate to come out. I can't let him know that. For a few seconds we stand in silence, staring at each other. His face is so close to mine, I can feel his heavy and frustrated breath on my face. I will not be the first person to speak.

'Now, are you going to sit back down or am I going to have to throw you back onto that bed?' He asks, I assume that was a joke, but I really wouldn't put it past him. Silently, I slowly back away and sit back down on my bed.

'I'm going to get some milk,' I say to him, breaking out of my thoughts before I can think too much. He grunts in response, too distracted to use real words.

Thankfully, Louie listened to the instruction I gave him at the café. Although, I am not sure how much of it he understands or what he thinks is going on. He's been threatening Gracie, telling her he will tell everyone that she's faking her memory loss and it's quite convincing. I know this because yesterday he said it to me, thinking I was her. I'm surprised how it easy it was for him to worm his way in, I guess that just shows how pathetic Gracie really is. I've really been trying to keep my distance from him; but it can be difficult since he spends most of his time here. When he thinks I'm Gracie, he doesn't really speak to me anyway. I don't blame him there, even if I could speak directly to Gracie, I wouldn't. She's so fucking boring. Thankfully his presence in the house has meant that Andy has kept his distance too.

I slip my coat on and open the front door. Now that I have Gracie distracted, it's finally time for me to attend to other things. It's quite warm today but the dull skies are threatening rain. I need to get back before the heavens open.

The high street is quiet as I walk down it, with only a few cars passing me. I suddenly get the feeling that someone is watching me. I can't help but feel suspicious just in case there's someone lurking. Someone like Jane, that's why I need to make sure.

Gracie

Disappearing for two years is hard, especially on your own. I had to rely on the help of some unsavoury people, some I didn't particularly end on good terms with. I put my trust into the wrong people and had to do some regretful things to get out of it.

A blue car pulls up next to me, relieving my suspicions. Nothing too unsavoury, just a nosey cow,

'Gracie,' Penny says rolling her window down. She is sitting in the driver's seat giving me what I assume is her best fake smile. I respond accordingly. It's a shame, I have managed to go this long without having to see her. It's a little disappointing that I am now faced to face with her after all this time of peace.

'Hi,' I say enthusiastically. She rolls her eyes at me. Her attitude doesn't surprise me, after all, I am the reason behind her and Gracie's issues. Unlike Gracie, I can't help but sniff out the fake bitches. I just helped Gracie see her true colours.

'Where are you off to?' She asks. I consider telling her to mind her own business but somehow, I don't think that will go down too well.

'The shop.' I say simply, trying to choose the fast-track option out of this conversation.

'I can give you a lift if you want?' She offers, I know she's not asking to be nice. I think back to the stranger danger video they used to show at school, the one that tells you not to get into cars with crazy ladies.

'No. I'm fine, it's just at the end of the road,' I point out.

'Funny you remember that?' She laughs to herself.

'Well, it's not rocket science,' I reply, 'we drive past it all the time'. I smile at her. My response silences her for a few heavenly seconds.

'You look like you're up to something,' she snaps.

'Ok,' I say slowly, fighting the urge to laugh in her face. 'Bye Penny.'

She hesitates before putting her window up and driving away. Thank God! What an awful woman, no wonder her husband left her. It makes me feel sorry for Andy, that is until he opens his mouth. Penny and Gracie were very close, that was until I came along. Penny is the kind of person who likes you until you disagree with her, or if you do something that she disagrees with. And I did both of those things. Then, their relationship started to suffer for it. Poor Gracie didn't know what had hit her. Penny started treating us terribly and now Gracie hates her too. I personally think I did Gracie a favour there, got her out of that control freak's control. Someone really ought to help Andy out with that too.

I watch as her car gets further away from me, I can still see her eyes glued on me through her mirrors. I stand and wave until the car is fully out of sight and then start to walk again. I wouldn't put it past her if she followed me. I know she is looking for anything to get Connor on her side. It's kind of pathetic that she cares that much about something that has literally nothing to do with her.

I walk up the street and to the shop. I stop at the entrance and look around. The streets are empty with only a few cars passing. It's 2pm on a weekday, people have better things to be doing. I walk down the side of the shop and around the corner. I take one last glance around to be safe and make sure there isn't anyone near who could watching me, someone like Penny. I pinch the handle of the phone box and pull the door open before stepping in. Ew. It smells like piss in here, I don't want to even imagine the kind of things that have gone on in here. I force those thoughts to the back of my head and try to concentrate on why I have come in the first place. I keep my breathing to a minimum and rummage in my jeans pocket for the change I took from the kitchen side. I pull out a £1 coin and put it into the phone box. I cover my finger with my sleeve and start dialling the number I have been trying so hard to remember.

The line beeps as it waits for someone to answer on the other end. I listen and wait, expecting to hear an answer phone message or something. I wait to her voice, her promise to call back but nothing. The phone finally just disconnects.

What does that mean? Has someone disconnected the phone? Is the answering machine full? Did someone decline the call? Did someone find her? I feel my heart beginning to race as I start to panic. I need to calm down.

The phone disconnecting could mean anything. It doesn't confirm or deny what might've happened...

Gracie

J

*

'I got us some milk,' my dad says walking into the kitchen. I'm standing at the sink, soaking Louie's coffee mug that he so kindly left on the living room floor. I turn around to speak to him.

'Gracie already got some,' Louie says before I can. That wasn't what I was going to say because I didn't get any. My dad's eyes shoot to Louie, then straight at me. I can tell by his face that he's disappointed that Louie is here. It's safe to say that he has never liked him.

'No, I didn't,' I say slowly. He's been here all day and neither of us have left the house.

'Yes, you did,' Louie replies slowly, looking at me as if I'm stupid. What the hell is he talking about? My dad walks over to the fridge and opens it. Both Louie and I watch in silence as he pulls out a full carton of milk. What on earth?

'Seems like you did,' my dad says. I stare at the milk carton in his hand. I know I didn't get that. I look over to Louie and he looks amused. Did he get it? Is he trying to mess with me? Trying to make me look crazy? I wouldn't put that past him but what would be the point? How could he have known that my dad was going to come in with milk. Besides, he hasn't left the sofa today, I know that.

Was it me? Did I go and get the milk today? My brain runs over everything I did today and leaving the house wasn't one of them. I know I didn't, but where did that milk come from? It definitely wasn't there this morning. I look over to my dad and he's staring at me, giving me that look of concern. It's as if he's waiting for an explanation, but I don't have one.

'Don't worry Gracie, you're suffering from memory loss, things like this are bound to happen.' he says reassuringly. I nod slowly, trying to take in his reassurance but it's not working. There is no memory loss, this isn't bound to happen, there must be something else going on. I feel my brain starting to scan through every possibility, all my thoughts are whirring away and—

'Anyway, ya freak, I'm off, I'll see you later,' Louie says loudly interrupting my panic. He stretches and reaches up to the ceiling. Both my dad and I watch as he walks out of the kitchen and listen as Louie leaves. Neither of us say anything until we hear the front door shut. The tension dissolves as soon as we hear the click of the door closing.

'So, what's for dinner?' I ask trying to push away any fear that I'm feeling and pull myself up onto the kitchen counter.

'I was thinking pasta,' my dad replies. Pasta again. I am starting to get sick of it, but I can't knock him; I can see he's trying so hard.

'Great,' I reply enthusiastically, watching him finally put the mysterious milk carton back into the fridge.

'Have you spoken to Andy at all? He's been asking after you,' he says sounding hopeful. He's just trying to make me feel better, I know that Andy hasn't been asking about me, Andy doesn't care anymore.

'I haven't heard from him at all,' I explain, watching him walk to the sink and fill the kettle with water. I wish I would hear something from him, his silence is killing me. I hate that he hates me right now.

'I was actually talking to Penny earlier and she said she saw you,' he says casually, changing the painful subject I assume.

'Oh really? Where?' I ask.

'She saw you walking down the street,' he explains.

'That's odd,' I say. 'It must've been someone else, I haven't left the house today.'

'She said you spoke,' he adds with a touch of accusation.

'Weird,' I say. Penny hates me and I have no idea why. It was as if one day she just decided she didn't like me anymore and randomly turned against me. It was sad because we were so close, but it was her choice to turn against me and there was nothing I could do about it. After seeing her true colours, I wasn't too bothered about reconciling with her anyway. She's been trying to catch me out ever since I came back so I am not surprised she would make up a lie like this. I'm still convinced Louie was tricking me with the milk but, there is no way I would forget a complete conversation with someone. 'Anyway,' I say noticing the time. 'I need to get ready for later, call me down when it's ready,' I say pushing myself off the counter and towards the kitchen door.

'Wait!' His voice pounces on me, 'I want to speak to you about something,' he says quickly. I stop and turn around, taking my seat back on the counter. His face has suddenly gone all red and blotchy. He seems very uncomfortable, it's very strange. 'So, there's something I have been meaning to tell you, I've not kept it from you, I just wanted to wait until the right time,' he explains with his hands. I nod; encouraging him to speak and waiting for him to reveal his big news.

'I have a girlfriend,' he says after a painful few seconds of silence. I feel my face drop, that was the last thing I was expecting him to say. His words have seemed to relieve him from whatever he was feeling because now a cheesy smile has spread across his face.

'Since when?' I say suddenly feeling defensive but trying to hide it.

'For a few months now,' he explains, blissfully unaware of the thoughts in my head.

Gracie

'Right,' I say slowly. I don't know how I am supposed to react to his. How could he meet someone so soon and move on so quickly? It hasn't even been that long; he clearly didn't want to waste any time. How long has this been going on? How long after did it start?

'You will meet her soon,' he adds. I try to rationalise and think logically. But I can't, I'm angry at him. It's only been a few weeks. How could he? How could he move on so quickly?

'Ok,' I say simply, pushing the only safe words out of my mouth. He looks as if he is about to say something else, but I can't just sit here and listen to him gush about this woman for any longer. How could he want to be with someone else? 'Can I go now?' I ask.

I don't wait for him to answer. I push myself off the counter and fall onto my feet. Every emotion is attacking me, but I can't feel it. I am not allowed; it would be too obvious. I try to tell myself that it's been two years and it's ok for him to move on, but it feels wrong. It sounds selfish, but I'm finding it hard to believe that he had a life without us.

The pub hasn't changed at all in the last two years, which is nice, at least something has stayed the same. It still has its old and dusty furniture, it's ugly, stained carpet and that stench of man and beer. When we arrived, the room went silent and everyone was staring at me. I guess that's what you get when you come back from the dead. Did they all see my name on the news, my face on posters,

256

talked about me with their friends? Is that why they are all looking at me like that?

Louie and I were served straight away at the bar. He ordered himself a beer and a glass of wine for me; without asking me what I wanted. I hate white wine, but I'll drink it for an easier life. He then went over and sat down with his friends and has left me standing on my own; they were all staring too. I don't mind, I think I'd rather be on my own then with him anyway. People are going to stare regardless of if I am on my own or not. I sigh, looking around.

'Gracie?' A voice says behind me. I turn around to see a small blonde with a nervous smile on her face.

'Hi,' I say quietly recognising her face.

'Do you remember me?' She asks with a hopeful smile. It's fake, I can tell. I'm not sure this girl is capable of anything genuine.

'No,' I lie. Dianne, we are not friends, never have been.

'Oh,' she says disappointed. Fake again. 'I'm Dianne. How are you? We were all so worried!' She says smiling sweetly at me.

'I'm good thanks. Who are you?' I ask, smiling sweetly back.

'We were best friends at school, I was so devastated when you disappeared,' she is speaking slow to me, as if I am a small child.

257

Gracie

'Oh really?' I say, all lies.

'We're all so glad you made it home safe,' she says.

'Thanks.'

'So, you're here with Louie?' She asks with a sour look on her face.

'Yes,' I reply.

'Well, I am really shocked about that. I thought you and Andy would have gotten back together,' she explains. 'After you went missing, Andy was inconsolable for nearly a year, I don't even think Louie batted an eyelid about the whole situation.' Nosey cow.

'Right.' I say slowly, not knowing what to say to her. I know she is only here because she's nosey, if it wasn't for my 'memory loss' then there is no way she would have the balls to even approach me, let alone tell me how much she missed me. I look over to Louie and see that his eyes are locked on us.

'After you disappeared Lo—' Louie walks over to us and yanks me towards him before she can even finish her sentence.

'Shut up and mind your own business, Dianne.' Louie spits at her pulling me away and out of the pub. I stumble after him. If everyone wasn't staring when we walked in, they definitely are now. I feel my cheeks go red and I try to keep my eyes on the floor. Louie finally let's go when we're in the car park.

'What were you doing talking to her?' He asks.

'Why did you pull me away?' I ask, that reaction was completely unnecessary.

'Because that girl is horrible,' he replies. 'She's just trying to cause trouble; I don't like you talking to her.'

'Why?' I ask. What's his issue with her? I don't remember there ever being one.

'It doesn't matter why! Let's go back inside, and you can stand with me,' he says. I am humiliated already, I couldn't imagine walking back in there and sitting with him, after everyone has just watched him drag me out.

'No. I'd rather go home,' I say. I am sick of him treating me this way. What was the point of him even inviting me here tonight if all he was going to do was leave me standing there on my own? His grip on my wrist tightens and he pulls me towards him.

'Come on,' he says aggressively.

'No,' I say loudly. His eyes are heavy on mine. He finally lets go of my wrist and I fall down onto the floor.

'Suit yourself,' he says after a few seconds, he looks fed up. How could he be fed up when he's the one forcing this? He turns around and walks away, finally leaving me alone.

Gracie

I know he thinks that I'm going to follow him in, but not this time. As much as I need him to keep my secret, there is no way I can walk back in there after that. I stand up and wipe the gravel off the back of my legs. I just want to go home. I know Louie must be after something and whatever that is, he hasn't got it yet. So, I'm guessing he won't expose my secret for just leaving.

The pub is in the middle of nowhere. It's way too far to walk. I can't call my dad; he'd lose his shit with Louie and I don't need that right now. I reach into my bag and pull out my phone. I look down and realise that this isn't my phone. I look at the screen and see a picture of a blonde woman standing with my dad. I must've picked up my dad's phone by accident and this must be her. I click on his contacts and find Andy's name.

'Connor, what's up?' I hear Andy's voice on the other end of the line, he sounds good and happy to be speaking to my dad. I hope he doesn't hang up when he finds out it's me.

'It's me,' I say timidly.

'What do you want Gracie?' His voice changes quickly, it's so stern and so blunt now. He's never spoken like this to me before. I suddenly lose control of all my emotions and the tears I have been holding back feel too heavy to hold anymore.

'Andy,' I start crying, feeling pathetic. 'Can you come and pick me up please?'

'Yes,' he says quickly, all the anger in his voice disappears. 'Where are you?'

'The Rose,' I say. 'I'm going to start walking,' I hang up before he can change his mind and put the phone back into my bag.

After a long 10 minutes of walking, I feel headlights shine on my back. I keep walking, holding my concentration on the white lines on the side of the road. The car slows down and stops next to me.

'You're walking the wrong way,' the voice says as the window rolls down. I look into the car and smile when I see Andy's face. 'Come on, get in,' he says reaching over and opening the passenger door for me.

He watches as I slowly climb into the car. As soon as I sit down, his familiar scent hits me and makes me realise just how much I have missed him. I look over to him and he is just sat there staring at me, as if he's waiting for me to say something. I give him a weak smile; I know I should say something. He deserves some kind of explanation, but I can't tell him the truth. I turn and look forward; he stares for a few seconds more before putting the car into gear. I rest my head on the window and the car pulls away. There is so much I want to say to him, but I know now is not the time. I need to sort myself out.

'What happened?' Andy asks finally breaking the silence. I knew he wouldn't last long.

'Louie was just being a bit of a dick, so I decided to come home,' I explain turning to look at him. He flinches at the mention of Louie's name. His cheek bones tense up and he tightens his grip on the steering wheel. His eyes are glued to the road in front of him and the tension rises.

'Why do you have your dad's phone?' He asks.

'I must've picked it up by accident or something, it was in my bag when I was looking for my phone.' I explain. 'Sorry should I have not called?' I ask feeling uncomfortable.

'No, I'm glad you called,' he says after a few seconds, he gives me a reassuring smile.

'It's probably good that I had it, you wouldn't have answered if you saw it was me.' I point out.

'Why would you say that?' He asks irritated. 'I will never not answer your call.'

'Hardly,' I snort. He turns to look at me, but I look away. I don't want to have this fight right now with him. I turn my attention to the window again.

'So, why was he being a dick?' He asks changing the subject, clearly sensing that it's not the right time to talk about the past couple of days. His question is so casual and I can tell he is trying to play it cool, but I know he's fishing for information.

'Andy please,' I beg. 'Can you just take me home and we can maybe talk about it tomorrow?' I suggest.

'Ok, yea, that's fine.' I hear the smile in his voice.

I know that I love him and I know it's him I want to be with. I just need to find a way to tell him, to explain to him all that has happened.

Gracie

8

*

I'm sitting in the living room, impatiently trying to distract myself by watching the TV. I am starving and waiting for Connor to get back with the takeaway. He is taking ages and I'm sick of waiting. He drives like an old woman, which is probably why it's taking so long.

When the doorbell rings I jump up in excitement, not caring that Connor has forgotten his keys and run towards the front door.

'Oh,' I open the door, disappointed it's not my food. Louie is standing on the other side of the door looking sheepish. I should think so, he should be looking guilty. I don't even know how but Gracie managed to get hold of Andy last night. There's nothing on her phone showing me how it happened but somehow, she ended up in his car and not where she was supposed to be, with Louie. He literally did the opposite of what I asked him to do. I really thought I could trust him with this. He could've really messed things up for me.

'Hello babe,' he says confidently, any guilt that was on his face washes away. He's pretending that last night didn't happen.

'What are you doing here?' I ask already feeling irritated.

'I thought I'd come here and get your apology for leaving last night.'

'For what?' I ask almost choking on his audacity.

'Just say sorry and then we can move on from this,' he says impatiently. He thinks I'm Gracie, clearly.

'No,' I say bluntly, my irritation turns to anger.

'Gracie, if you break up with me, then I'll have no choice but to tell everyone your little secret,' he smiles. 'There is no point in denying it, we both know what's going on here.'

'Oh really,' I say, amused by his little act, it doesn't work on me.

'Yes!' He shouts. Now he's getting angry that I'm not folding.

'I think I'll take my chances,' I wink, trying to wind him up. I want him to feel like I do. He stares at me for a few seconds, his eyes are on mine, it's intense. He's trying to break me, but it's not going to work.

'Gracie!' He says, after finally realising it's me. His face lights up and his whole presence changes.

'I don't know what you're talking about,' I say simply. I don't want to speak to him right now, I can't, he let me down.

'I was wondering when I was going to see you again,' he says taking a step closer to me, I flinch and take a step back. 'I've missed you.'

'I don't know what you're talking about,' I say again.

'Don't be like this, I did what you said,' he says defensively, starting to look lost. His eyes attack mine and I look away from him. 'Gracie.'

'What?' I snap, not able to take his intense eye contact for any longer.

'Where have you been?' He asks. 'What is going on? How is there two of you? Who is she?' His questions fly through me.

'I don't know what you're talking about,' I repeat for the third time. Involving him was a mistake, I don't know what I was thinking.

'Are you fucking serious?' He shouts, suddenly losing it completely.

When I look up at him, I feel that gut punching feeling in my stomach. What am I doing to him? He is going mad with all of this. And it makes me want to tell him everything. He feels safe to me. But then I hear Connor outside and before either of us can recover, he walks through the front door and freezes when he sees us standing there. My chance is gone. When I look back to

Louie, he just looks angry now, furious with me and what I've put him through these past couple of days.

'Are you going to tell him, or am I?' Louie says all of a sudden. My stomach drops and the air suddenly feels harder to breath in.

'Tell me what?' Connor says, putting the bag of food on the floor and slipping off his coat. Time feels like it's passing so quickly but painfully slowly too. I look at Louie and everything in me is telling him to look at me, but his eyes are fixed on Connor. I start to panic. Everything is about to unfold right in front of my eyes and I have no control over it.

'Gracie has been lying to you this whole time.' My heart starts to pound and I can feel my body starting to sweat. Louie doesn't fully know the truth so God knows what he's going to come out with, but what if he says something? And then Connor realises that I'm not her and tries to mute me. 'There is two of them,' I cringe, trying to think of ways to diffuse this. How can I turn this a— 'She has a secret twin,' Louie announces and all my thoughts freeze. A secret twin? What? I over look at Connor and the look on his face softens. My anxiety disappears as relief washes through my body.

'Twins,' Connor repeats looking amused.

'Right,' I say, laughing loudly, mocking Louie. I didn't know what Louie understood about the situation, but I definitely didn't think it was this. Twins? Really?

'Maybe you should go,' Connor suggests politely, although I know it's not a suggestion. 'It's our dinner time and there's not enough food for you.' He says folding his lips into an awkward line.

Neither Louie nor I move and after a few more seconds of awkward silence, Connor picks up the bag of food and walks into the kitchen. I almost want to follow him in there and leave Louie here, but he deserves more than that. When the kitchen door shuts, the look on Louie's face makes me feel sick.

'Gracie, you're making me crazy,' he whispers. 'Please, just let me in, tell me what's going on here. You know how I feel about you; you know I can help.'

'Louie, you have just showed me that I can't trust you,' I say sadly.

'Please Gracie,' he begs. The look on his face is heart breaking, I should've never involved him in this again, it's made things more complicated, harder.

'I made it all up,' I say, trying to reject all this feeling inside of me. I need to use my brain and nothing else.

'Made it up? Made what up?' He asks.

'It's been me all along.' I say.

'Not possible,' he replies, shooting me down. 'I don't believe that.'

'Believe it or not, but you said it yourself, you're going crazy.' I'm trying to say everything and anything that will get me out of this situation and him free of all of this. Bringing him into this was a mistake, I should've known from the last time.

'Gracie, please.'

'Louie, I was bored, that's all,' I say trying to sound uninterested.

'No. I don't believe that for a second,' he says. 'If all this a game, why did you come back then? To trick me, to mess me around? No, it's bullshit. There's something going on here, I know it.'

'Believe what you want, I don't care,' I say. He takes a step forward towards me and for a second, I think he's going to hit me, but instead his hands are on my face pulling me towards his lips. He kisses me and my body responds without my brain's permission. We fall into familiarity. It feels good to have something I have been depriving myself from for so long, it feels good after feeling so alone. His arms move away from my face and down my back, holding me tight against him. I can't move but I don't want to, for the first time in a long time, I feel safe.

'You do care, I know you do.' He whispers pulling away from me. I feel lost, his lips aren't there anymore. He's still holding me close. I can feel his warm breath on my face. 'Let me in. I love you and I know you love me too; I can help. You don't have to do whatever this in alone. Please.' I look up at him, wanting to tell him. I want him to help me but I know he can't. It's not possible. It wouldn't work, it didn't work between us two years ago and nothing's changed. I can't put him through anymore of this shit, it's not fair. He deserves more than this, we both do.

'No,' I whisper, blinking away the stray tears and holding back the rest of them. His hands go back to my face and I don't want to move, but this can't go on. I should've never dragged him back into this.

'I can't beg you to love me anymore. I can't keep chasing something that won't let me catch it. Just give me anything, something to hold on to. Please,' he begs and I feel my heart break. I know how hard it would've been for him to say that, how much those words mean to the both of us. I lift my hand up to my face and catch a stray tear which I promise to myself is the last and take a step away from him.

'There's nothing to hold on to,' I say quickly before I can stop myself. 'I don't love you. Like I said it's all been a game.' I lie surprised by the sound of my own voice; it doesn't sound like me at all.

'Fine,' he says. My words instantly change him and just like that I've lost him. Everything he just said means nothing now. 'I'll go. You've fucked with me too much. You're the one who's fucking crazy.' I know he's trying to hurt me, just like I just hurt him. 'You're a selfish bitch. It's easier to hate you than to love you anyway.'

He opens the front door and I watch as he walks away from me. I can feel the ache rise in my throat. I try to push all that feeling away, I can't cry yet. He stops after a few steps.

'I know you're lying,' he says, still facing away from me. 'But I've done everything I can. I'm done.' He can't even look at me. 'But if it ever comes to it, I'm here.'

I slam the door and lean back on it, needing it to support me. The pressure in my chest spreads through my body, making it hard to even stand up. I slowly lower myself onto the floor and let the hot tears fall from my eyes before they burn me. I struggle to catch my breath and try to steady it, but I feel suffocated. I hold my breath and force myself to stop. I can't do this; I can't feel this right now.

I quickly stand up, push my hair behind my ears and wipe my eyes. I look at my reflection in the mirror and tell myself that I can feel later, when I'm free.

'What was that about?' Connor asks as I walk into the kitchen.

'I honestly have no idea, he just snapped when I told him it was over,' I say, trying not to face him directly.

I sit down at the kitchen table, grateful that Connor is distracted with taking our food out of the bag. I watch him as he carefully placed each container on the table. I can't help but think about Louie, where is he going now, what is he doing? All I can think about is him getting into his car and driving away, hating me. But what else was I supposed to do? If things were different, then maybe we could've had a chance. But this is real life. We were doomed from the beginning; you can't build a real relationship on secrets. The tears start to vibrate behind my eyes again and I stop myself, blinking them away before Connor notices. He looks up at me and his face falls, he knows somethings wrong. Before he can say anything, his phone starts vibrating on the table. I'm thankful for the distraction and quickly start grabbing the food in front of me.

'Oh, crap!' Connor says staring at his phone screen.

'What is it?' I ask opening the container with the egg fried rice in it.

'Andy went over to Louie's earlier and started an argument with him,' he explains.

'And,' I say filling my plate with food and ignoring the sting of Louie's name.

'Well, Louie didn't like that and now Andy's pretty hurt,' he explains. 'Did Louie mention anything when he was here?'

'No,' I say, 'he wasn't here for that long,' and Andy is pretty irrelevant to the both of us.

'I told Penny we'd be over there right away,' he says walking to the back door. I watch as he starts sliding on his shoes. Seriously? I look at our fresh and hot takeaway lying out on the table. It looks so good and I'm so hungry. 'Let's go,' he says staring at me impatiently.

I take one last look at the food. It looks so good. Why does Andy have to ruin everything?

Penny opens the door and instead of being her normal, irritating self, she just looks drained. She even avoided giving me the evil eye, which shows something is up. She steps aside and invites us in. I follow Connor into the living room and feel Penny's eyes follow me as I walk past her. The living room is dark with only a few dim lamps lighting it up. Andy is lying on the sofa, tucked under a light blanket, Penny's handiwork I'm guessing.

'How is he?' Connor asks turning to Penny.

'It looks a lot worse than it actually is,' she explains, glaring at me. I know she'll be blaming me for this. I look at Andy's face, it's a little bruised, clearly not worth missing out on dinner then because it doesn't look bad at all. I am starving.

'I took him to the hospital and they said that he just needs to rest, that's why I didn't call you straight away,' she explains, her eyes are still on mine, giving me that accusing look that I've seen so many times before. And did she really need to take him to the hospital after getting punched in the face? *Smother* much? As if it's my fault. It in definitely nothing to do with me that her son is a moron, what did he expect going over there? A friendly hug and an apology? Idiot. 'They have given him some medication for the pain.' she explains. Andy's eyes shoot open and look straight up at me.

'Maybe we should leave these two to talk,' Connor says nudging me playfully. Please. No. Don't leave me alone with lover boy. I can't take it, especially after the day I've had. Penny nods, sending me a warning look before walking into the kitchen. Connor follows her giving me an encouraging look. Lord give me strength.

'Gracie,' Andy whispers, his words are clumsy and slurred.

'What!' I snap. I can't help but feel anger towards him, this is all his fault. If he wasn't so obsessed with Gracie, it would be easier to get rid of her and I'd actually get a chance to be me.

'Come closer,' he whispers again. I can barely hear him; he's mumbling like a child. I step closer and kneel down on the floor next to him.

'I'm so glad you came,' he says, 'I've missed you'.

'Why did you go over to Louie's?' I ask.

'Because it's all his fault,' he spits all over me, 'he manipulated you, made you hate me'. What a victim, if anything it's Andy's fault. If it wasn't for his refusal to let go of Gracie the last time, I wouldn't have had to leave.

The Way Back

'Louie didn't do anything, I chose him and not you,' I say simply. I hate him. I want my words to cut through him and destroy him. I want him to feel how I feel right now. 'You're pathetic, I will never love you.'

'So, this is all your fault!' I flinch as he shouts in my face. His voice echoes through the room.

The kitchen door flies open and I turn around to see Connor striding in. Penny follows closely, like a loyal little bitch.

'We should really let him have his rest,' Connor says standing between the two of us. 'The medication is making him act this way.'

'I don't know what I said to him to upset him,' I say standing up. 'I'm soooooo sorry,' I stare back at Penny, fighting the urge to smile. She glares back at me, if looks could kill...

'It's getting late now anyway,' Connor says putting his arm around me and unknowingly breaking the tension between Penny and me. My performance was obviously very believable to him. He ushers me out of the room and away from Penny's death stare.

At least now I can eat my Chinese.

After the worst night of sleep in my life, I spend the day in Gracie's room, trying to stay out of the way. It seems to be the only place where I can be left alone.

Anywhere else, Connor seems to be lurking about, asking me annoying questions about Andy or Louie. I don't want to talk about it, especially not with him. At least here, I can sit here and be myself. Pretending to be Gracie all the time is exhausting, especially when it's her fault I'm stuck here.

'Gracie!' Connor shouts up the stairs. I think about ignoring it, pretending I can't hear but I know that he will just keep shouting or worse come up and find me. Why can't I just be left alone? 'Can you come down for a second please?'

I sit up and groan loudly. I can't wait to get out of here in a few months so I can finally be left alone. I try to remind myself that I'm so close, but I can't get my hopes up like the last time, that's how I ended up putting my guard down.

I don't know how long I've been lying in this bed, but it's long enough for me to leave behind a Gracie sized dent in the bed. The room is dark and there's a weird smell, a few minutes out of the room might be a good idea. I drag my feet out of the room and down the stairs. As I get closer, I hear voices in the living room, it's Connors and a women's voice, I think. I hope to God it's not Penny.

I walk into the living room and everything freezes. My eyes shoot towards the other person in the room. I feel chills shoot down my whole body. I see a face that I will never forget. A face I never thought I'd see again. Black, almost blue hair, pale skin and the most evil, black eyes. I'm speechless.

'Gracie, this is Brenda,' Connor says. I look up at him and he has a cheesy smile spread across his face. Brenda. Who the fuck is Brenda? This is not Brenda. This is Jane.

The shock paralyses me. I can barely speak; my words feel too weak. I feel my brain working overtime, trying to think of a logical reason as to how she is here, but it can't settle. There are too many thoughts shooting around my brain. It's impossible, but she's here. Why? How? And with Connor?

'Tea?' She asks looking up at me. All the heat in my body rise to my face, my cheeks are on fire.

'We don't have any milk,' Connor points out. I look at him, he looks weird. The way he's sat in the chair, it's odd. His voice is much lower, much slower than usual.

'Well, then why don't you run out and get some,' she says, her tone pushes him down to the floor, making him look tiny but Connor just seems to just accept it. 'Gracie and I can get to know each other while you're gone,' she looks over to me and her menacing smile punctures me. No. He can't leave me here, alone with her. Connor's eyes meet mine, looking for confirmation.

'Sure,' I reply slowly, the words coming out before I can catch them.

'The sooner you leave, the sooner you'll be back,' Jane says placing her hands on Connor's shoulders and pushing him towards the door. They move slowly, almost lagged. Like a glitch. 'Gracie and I will be fine, won't we?'

She says, giving me a wicked look. I feel the lump in the
back of my throat getting bigger and bigger. Connor stands
there for a second, like he's hesitating, then he picks up his
keys from the coffee table.

Jane gestures for me to sit down next to her, where Connor
was sitting. My legs move without permission and
suddenly I am sat in the armchair. There's silence as we
wait for Connor to make his way out of the house.
Everything feels slower, it feels glitchy. I feel my cold
hands underneath my legs, the cold travels through my
hands and down my legs. I take a slow breath and smell it
again, the smell from my room. Is it me? It's not bad, but
it's not good either. The smell, it burns. But it feels
familiar.

My eyes lock onto Jane and she stares back. I don't want to
take my eyes off her, I learnt that I couldn't trust Jane the
hard way. She is sat there, completely relaxed, none of this
phases her. She looks good, healthy. The last time I saw
her, she was looking a lot worse. I didn't think that a quick
recovery was possible. She gives me a friendly smile and I
feel uncomfortable, this whole situation feels off. I can't
help but stare at her jumper, it's pink. I've never seen her
in anything other than black.

'What are you doing here?' I turn to Jane when I
hear Connor shutting the front door.

'Who am I speaking to?' She mouths.

'Gracie doesn't even know who you are!' I point out.

'Oh yeah,' she laughs. 'So, I'm glad it's you then.'

'What are you doing here?' I ask again.

'Are you surprised to see me?' She says raising her eyebrows, 'I can understand why, you probably thought I was dead. Most people don't survive a knife to the chest.'

'So what? You're with now Connor then?' I ask finally finding the words I want to use.

'Yes, I am,' she laughs. 'I'm surprised you've lasted this long, pretending to be her. So, what's your plan? I know you won't be staying, you always said you couldn't stand being here, stuck in her life,' she laughs. 'Are you going to move away and start a new life? Surely that's the only option.' I feel like I have just been punched in the stomach. Jane will ruin everything; she did the first time when I stupidly trusted her. Only for her to manipulate me and trap me in that stupid house. 'You thought that you'd finally got rid of me, you'll never be free.' I can't believe she is here, with Connor. It doesn't even make sense, how? Since when? I saw Jane every day in that house, there is no way she would've been able to start a relationship with him from so far away. None of this adds up.

'Is anyone in there?' Jane asks grabbing my attention and taunting me.

Gracie

'Uh what, yes,' I say, feeling myself focus on reality again.

'Oh no, have you changed?' She mouths again, as if Gracie wouldn't suspect anything from that if we had switched.

'No,' I say shaking my head at her, looking at her as if she's stupid. 'I'm fully in control,' I lie. Jane has caught me off guard and I can feel Gracie wanting to come out. It's been getting harder to keep her in recently.

Connor appears and saves me. I look up at him, he's holding a carton of milk in one hand and a packet of chocolate biscuits in the other. I stare at the packet in his hand. That was quick, it was too quick. It was impossible.

'Tea?' Connor says cheerfully.

'Go on then,' Jane says from the sofa, giving him a wicked smile. I try to focus on the milk, to make sense of what's happening.

'Everything ok?' He looks over to me.

'Yes,' I nod. Everything around me suddenly seems so, flat. I try to say something else, but my mouth feels numb. I can't sit here for any longer. I feel so far away. Gracie is fighting her way out and I don't think I can hold her off for much longer. 'Not fancying a tea though, I think I'm going to rest my eyes for a bit.' I manage to push the words out before standing up. Everything feels out of my control, like I have pins and needles in my whole body.

The Way Back

I don't know what's wrong with me. I have never felt this way before.

I manage to run up the stairs and into Gracie's room. I'm not sure how, my body and brain feel so disconnected. Every message I try to send to my body seems to get lost. I shut the door behind me and start to pace through the room. I have to concentrate, to stop her from coming out. My legs start to feel too wobbly. I sit down at her dressing table and try to control myself, calm my breathing. I hear Connor's voice downstairs and try to focus on it. His voice travels through to the kitchen and becomes too weak to focus on and hold my attention. I look up and try to put my focus onto my reflection. My skin starts to blur, I can feel myself distancing, getting further and further away. I need to stop it, it—

9

*

I'm staring at my reflection in the mirror. It takes me a second to realise, how did I get here? I look up at the clock on my wall and see its half one in the afternoon. The last thing I remember is going to sleep. I'm losing more and more memory now and blacking out for longer, what's happening to me? I notice a stray tear on my cheek, slowly falling down my face. I wipe it away and stare at it on my thumb. Why am I crying? What's happened? My stomach feels heavy and I'm anxious. I don't know what this is, or what's happened but it doesn't feel good. The feeling and need to get out of this house is overpowering.

I quickly slip a hoody over my head and walk out of my bedroom. I can hear my dad downstairs in the kitchen. As I walk down the stairs, I try to make sense of the anxiety that I'm feeling.

'Changed your mind about that cup of tea?' I turn to the voice; it's coming from the living room. I look into the room and see a lady sitting on the sofa. I don't know this woman, but I recognise her. She's the blonde woman from Cameron's phone.

'What?' I say confused. I suddenly realise who this woman is, I can't even look at her.

'Are you ok?' My dad asks as he walks out of the kitchen. He's holding two mugs; he reaches out and passes one of them to her. Then it clicks. This is why I am so uncomfortable, it's because she's here.

'Er, yes,' I say, trying to straighten my thoughts.

'Did you want a cup of tea then?' He asks slowly looking confused.

'Er, no.' I need to get out of this house. I can't be here right now. 'I am going to go and see Andy I think.'

'Ok,' he replies slowly.

I turn around and walk to the front door as quickly as I can. I am sweating. I shove my feet into my shoes and walk out the door. My heart is racing, I feel so awkward. She was just sat there in my living room, our living room.

After almost running here, I finally stop at Andy's front door. I haven't seen or spoken to him since he picked me up the other night. He said he'd call but never did. I need to see him and if he doesn't want to see me, then he is just going to have to tell me that to my face. I take a breath before knocking loudly on the front door. After a few seconds the opens the door, I feel relieved when I see it's him and not his mum. He smiles and steps into the light revealing a big bruise covering his face.

'Gracie,' he says beaming.

Gracie

'Your face,' I point out. It looks awful.

'It's gotten a lot better, hasn't it?' He says.

His question throws me. Better? It was worse? And I already knew about it? I nod, not being able to take my eyes off it. What happened to him?

'Can I come in?' I ask quietly, still distracted by his face.

'Yes, of course,' he says stepping aside to let me in. I walk past him and into the house, taking my shoes off at the door.

'Is your mum here?' I whisper.

'She's in the kitchen, but I think she's going out in a bit,' he explains.

'Can we go upstairs then? To talk?' I ask.

He nods. It feels so awkward between us, I hate it. I walk up the stairs and Andy follows closely behind. Neither of us say anything until we reach his room. When I open the door, I head straight over to his bed and sit down. He cautiously follows, sitting down but keeping his distance.

'Are you ok?' He asks slowly, his voice is deeper than normal.

'I'm fine,' I explain, 'it's just been a weird couple of days, my memory keeps blacking out'.

'I'm sure that's just a symptom of your memory loss, nothing you should be worrying about,' he says trying to reassure me. I'm sick of everyone saying that. There is no memory loss so there is no explanation as to why I can't remember things. I'm going mad, I can't tell anyone and there's nothing I can do to stop it.

'Yes, probably,' I agree with him, what else can I say?

'Why did you ignore my calls?' He asks. He's hurt, I can tell by the look in his eyes.

'I didn't, not on purpose. I didn't get any calls,' I explain.

He looks completely unconvinced, but I didn't get any calls from him. I was so upset when he didn't call me. I sigh loudly in frustration. I didn't come here to talk about this, the last thing I want to do is have an argument with him on whether he called me or not. I wait for him to say something, but he doesn't, he just sits there staring at me. The silence takes over, filling the room until I can't take it anymore. He's not going to make this easy for me.

'I'm sorry,' I blurt out, 'about everything'.

'I'm sorry too,' he replies immediately. I'm surprised, I didn't think he would say that; he hasn't done anything wrong.

'It's just been so hard, with coming back and stuff,' I explain, 'but I think I have now finally admitted to myself that it's you I want to be with and that I need to stop listening to the little voice in the back of my head saying no. I think I just ran back to Louie because I was scared,' I admit, which is half true, he doesn't need to know about the other half of Louie blackmailing me. Andy doesn't say anything, but he doesn't need to. The words are just falling out of me now, everything I have wanted to say since I came back. 'So I'm done hiding from my feelings because I'm scared or whatever is telling me not to,' I say nervously, feeling relieved that I'm finally saying it, that the words are coming out. It feels good. I look up and wait for him to say something, but he's still just sat there. The silence is sending my nerves through the roof. 'So, if you'll have me,' I say nervously, one final attempt to make him speak again.

His face is emotionless, there is no indication to what he's thinking or feeling right now. I wonder how long I should wait before saying something else, but I have said everything I need to. It's his turn now. After a few more awkward seconds, I consider walking out. Every second he doesn't say anything, the more stupid I feel.

'If I'll have you?' He finally breaks his silence and starts laughing. He's laughing? That is the last thing I expected from him. Why is he laughing? What does that mean? I feel the blood in my cheeks starting to boil with embarrassment. 'Gracie, you've always had me,' he smiles, 'you're so difficult but I wouldn't have you any other way'. I finally take a breath of relief. He reaches out and closes the space between us. He grabs my wrists and pulls me closer to him and lightly rests his hand on my cheek. 'But please, no more trouble, no more drama and no more games,' he warns. 'I can't take anymore.'

'I promise,' I reply, falling into his kiss.

10

*

I open my eyes, look up at the ceiling and realise that I am not in Gracie's bed. Where am I? I sit up and look around the room. This room is an actual dump, there are clothes all over the floor and— oh God! No, they are Gracie's clothes. That's her hoodie and there are those ugly jeans, inside out on the floor. Oh God! Please. I see someone in the corner of the room, their back is turned away from me, sitting at a desk, that better not be—

'You're awake,' Andy says spinning in his chair towards me. Fuck.

'Hi,' I reply awkwardly.

'Are you feeling better?' He asks.

'Yes,' I reply slowly, playing along. What is he talking about? 'I do.'

He smiles and stands up. He walks over to the bed and towards me, he's shirtless, wearing only a pair of grey joggers. Oh God, no Gracie! He sits down next to me and I try to move back. The headboard stops me from moving any further away from him.

'I'm glad you're feeling better,' he says leaning over and kissing my shoulder. My bare shoulder. The touch of his lips on my skin sends a repulsive chill down my spine. I suddenly feel very naked with only a vest top and my knickers covering me. Oh fuck. His kisses slowly make their way up my neck and along my jaw line.

'I should go,' I say pulling away from him. I crawl past him and off the bed. He turns and watches me as I stand up and rush to the jeans on the floor. Never did I think I would be so grateful to see these ugly things again. I quickly pull the jean legs the right way before throwing my legs into them and pulling them up to my waist.

'Gracie,' Andy says, his face is all scrunched up looking confused. I ignore him and grab my hoodie. I pull it over my head and spot Gracie's bra on the floor by the door. I cringe picking it up and shove it into the big pocket on the hoodie. What has Gracie done? She can't be fucking trusted for a second. 'Gracie,' Andy repeats himself as I open his bedroom door.

'It's ok,' I say, not really knowing what to say to him, I just need to get out. I walk out and rush down the stairs, he follows me.

'Gracie,' he says again as I'm slipping on my shoes. 'Why are you in such a rush?'

'I have a lot to do today,' I lie, opening the front door. He places his hand on the door and pushes it shut it before I can squeeze out. The slam of the door startles me but I don't show him that.

'Ok, well maybe I can come and see you later?' He asks.

'Sure,' I nod, knowing that will not be happening. He smiles down at me. Before I can escape, he leans in and his puckered lips attack mine. His cold, soggy lips touch me and he gently pushes me against the door. The doorframe hits my head and I feel it digging into my skull. I don't know what he's trying to prove by kissing Gracie like this but it's not doing anything for me. This whole experience is traumatising. I close my eyes and start to count down the seconds to distract myself from the horror that is unfolding right on my face. When he finally pulls away, he looks down at me, giving me a funny look.

'Gracie,' he says quietly.

'What?' I ask irritated. I just want to leave.

'Come on Grace, give me a break with all of this hot and cold shit, I can't stand it anymore.'

'Hmm,' I say, his nickname for her makes me cringe. I wonder what more I could possibly do for him to get the message, I have literally run away from him, is that not a good enough hint for him?

'I know you, stop putting on this front that you don't care.' He reaches up and rests his hand on my cheek.

'I don't care,' I say, taking his hand and moving it away from me. I just want this conversation to be over, so I can leave.

'If you really didn't care, then why did you come here yesterday?' He asks, probably because Gracie is a fucking idiot who clearly cannot keep her legs shut for more than two seconds.

'I was bored.' I say using the words I know are going to hurt him the most. He takes a step back from me and for a second, I see the hurt on his face. 'Andy, maybe if you stopped making it so easy to walk all over you, then one day you'd be able to find someone just as pathetic as you to love, instead of someone who is way out of reach.'

'I, uh,' he stutters.

'Take my advice or leave it, it doesn't make much difference to me anyway,' I say, seeing the opportunity to get out. He's distracted by my words. I quickly reach behind me, open the door and slip out the small gap. 'See ya.'

I get out of there and home as quickly as I can. What an idiot! I can't leave that little slag alone for a second, it took her no time at all to run into Andy's bed. She very nearly ruined everything. I can't have Andy obsessing over Gracie, that's why I had to stage the whole 'disappearance' in the first place. He was never going to let her go, not even after the cheating or the lies. Eugh, if I'm not careful, I am going to be stuck living Gracie's pathetic life forever. The anger bubbles inside me. It's fine, I tell myself. I saved it. If that boy has any self-respect, he'll stay away from now on.

Gracie

I put my key in the front door and open it. When I walk through the door, Connor is just standing there holding a mug and staring at me. Was he just standing there waiting for me? No wonder Gracie is such a melt if this is what her family is like.

'Gracie, you're back,' Connor says. Good eye Captain Obvious.

'Yep,' I reply bluntly, wanting out of the conversation and into the safety of Gracie's room. What is it with all of these melts trying to talk to me today?

'Are you ok?' He asks, slowly and cautiously.

'Yes,' I reply wondering if that's the right answer, the one he wants to hear.

'Ok, good,' he replies. I take a step forward thinking the conversation is over when he starts speaking again. Ugh! 'It's just that you left so quickly yesterday I was worried.'

'Oh, I just had plans I was late for,' I lie.

'Well Brenda had to leave early this morning, but she will be back soon,' he explains. Oh. Fuck. I forgot about fucking Jane. Andy's gross naked body clearly distracted me from the real issue.

'Ok,' I say simply.

'Look Gracie, if—'

'It just freaked me out a bit,' I lie, a quick excuse for a quick solution. This is what he wants me to say. He wants me to share my *'feelings'*, it's the only way I am going to get out of this conversation.

'Ok,' he replies slowly, 'I just want to check though that you're okay with her being here?' You mean the woman who I tried to kill and is now here to return the favour?

'Uh yeah!' I reply enthusiastically, immediately realising I'm being too much.

'I'm happy to talk about it if you want to, whenever you want,' he offers.

Ok Connor. Your Girlfriend is a psychopath who took advantage of me when I tried to run away, then she kept me locked in a house for two years for no good reason and acted like a raging bitch the few times I did see her.

'Thanks,' I smile at him. 'Right now, I think I just want to get in the shower.' And wash Andy's gross germs off me.

'Ok, no problem,' he replies awkwardly stepping out of my way. I walk past him and up the stairs quickly before he can say anything else.

'I'm going to the pub later, so if you want to invite Andy round for some company, that might be a nice idea,' he shouts up the stairs after me.

'Yea, maybe,' I shout back. Maybe not.

Gracie

11

*

I wake up and reach out next to me. I open my eyes and sit up when I don't feel him. He's not there, I'm not in his bed, I'm in mine. I sit up, trying to push down the panic. I see my phone on the bedside table and grab it. When the screen lights up, it confirms everything.

It's Saturday morning. The last thing I remember is going to sleep on Thursday night. I've lost more than a whole day and I don't know what's happened in between. Before I completely lose it, I let my logic take over to try and think of an answer.

This isn't a game anymore, there is something wrong with me and I'm done trying to cover it up. I need to find out what's happening and stop it. I need to finally tell my dad the truth. I throw my phone down and pull myself out the bed.

When I open my bedroom door, I see a woman standing at the end of the hallway. This must be Brenda. She is wearing my dad's dressing gown. She looks up and smiles at me.

'Morning Gracie!' She says casually.

I suddenly feel my stomach turn and all the blood rush to my face.

12

*

I open my eyes and look around confused. We have never changed this quickly before, without any warning. I look in front of me and see Jane is standing at the end of the hallway. She's wearing Connor's dressing gown and is smirking at me. I take a breath and try to hide the fact that I feel so caught off guard, I can't show her that. Jane feeds off weakness.

I stare back, giving her the look of *'what'*. She loudly laughs to herself, at me. Then I smell it again, that burning smell. But this time, it's overwhelming, suffocating me and burning my nostrils. I look around, trying to see where it's coming from when I see Jane pulling something from behind her back.

A gun. I freeze. She still hasn't said anything. Her face is full of amusement as she lifts it up and points it at me. My feet are stuck to the ground, I can't move. She pulls the trigger and everything just disappears.

'Gracie,' I open my eyes to see Connor leaning over me.

'She shot me,' I whisper to him, opening my eyes. I look around and see that I am lying in a hospital bed. Great, back at square one.

'Shot you?' He asks, giving me a strange but worried look. 'No, Gracie you collapsed,' I heard the gun, I felt the bullet, I saw the blood. He pauses for a second before continuing, 'this might come as a shock to you, but we think it was a hallucination,' Connor explains.

'It felt so real,' I argue.

'I know it did, but you're ok, you weren't shot,' he explains. I look down, I am still wearing my pyjamas and there is no blood. I lift my pyjama top. My stomach is bare, there isn't anything on it. I can't even feel the pain anymore. There's nothing there. Jane must've done something to me, that's the only explanation to all of this. Jane? Where is she now? What has she said to Connor? 'Gracie,' Connor says trying to get my attention, 'since you came back, we have been monitoring you. I have been speaking with doctors, discussing your blackouts, your behaviour and all the things you have been experiencing.'

'And.' I say.

'Gracie, they have diagnosed you with a dual personality disorder.' Ding, Ding, Ding. Tell me something I don't know Connor; like where your fucking psycho girlfriend has gone.

'What?' I say thinking carefully and acting confused. I need to focus. If he realises that I'm not Gracie, it's over.

'You experienced a massive amount of trauma when you went missing and this is how you coped with it, but we can help you.' Incorrect, but I'll let him roll with it. I've been around a lot longer than he thinks.

'I don't understand,' I say weakly, playing the part.

'It's ok, I know that this is confusing, but the doctor will be able to talk you through it and explain it.'

I nod, trying to stay calm and pulling my best feel sorry for me face. That's exactly what Gracie would be doing right now. It's only a matter of time until they'll start trying to get rid of me. Connor wouldn't want some parasite living in his precious Gracie's head.

A blonde lady appears at the door, looking into the room.

'Thank God you're ok Gracie,' the lady says. Who the fuck is this? How does she know my name? I've never seen this woman before in my life. 'Connor, I am just going outside to make a phone call. I just wanted to let you know that I'm back. No sign of Penny yet though,' she explains. Good news then.

'Thanks Brenda,' Connor says. I feel my veins freeze. Brenda? That's Brenda? That doesn't make any sense. Brenda was Jane. She had black hair not blonde. She threatened me, she shot me.

But she didn't.

There was nothing there.

Connor was right, I did imagine it.

Gracie

There's a sinking feeling inside of me, a realisation. The memory of it suddenly unravels, the sight, the sound, how it felt and even the smell. What's real? And what isn't? The smell, that weird, familiar smell. I remember it when I first smelt it. The day I met Jane…

No. It can't have been. Jane has to have existed. Otherwise, who was keeping me in that house all this time? The panic in me rises and I can feel my heart starting to race, I can feel my pulse in my brain.

No, it can't. I would've never done that to myself. If it wasn't me, then who? Not pathetic, little Gracie? It couldn't be.

Oh. My. God. Of course. She started this whole thing, the memory loss. No wonder she went along with it so easily and only really questioned it once. Every action, every comment she made, even her thoughts were planned, she knew that I knew what was going on. She played me. That bitch. Gracie wasn't easy, she was clever. That's why it was so easy for Louie to get his way in, she knew my feelings for him, it was a distraction for me. She knew exactly what she was doing when she threw herself at Andy at any given second and her mum, she already knew. How did I not see that? It barely affected her.

I can't do this right now, I can't panic. Connor knows too much already. I need to stop. I need to get out of here before either they stop me and trap me here forever or Gracie gains control again. If I want to get out of this, I need to chill, swallow everything I am feeling and calm down.

'I know I should have so many questions, but I feel like my brain is completely scrambled. I'm so hungry, am I allowed to eat?' I ask looking up towards him.

'Yes, I think getting some food into your system is a good idea,' he replies agreeing with me.

'Would you mind getting me a sandwich and a drink please?' I ask.

'There's some orange juice here,' he says picking up a plastic jug.

'Erm, I don't really want that right now,' I say, 'can you get me something else please?'

'No problem,' he says standing up, kissing me on the forehead and walking out of the room.

I jump up as soon as he is out of sight. I need to get out now. If it was Gracie this whole time controlling me, that means that this is what she wanted, for me to end up in here. That's why it was me waking up here, not her. She knows that they will get rid of me, giving her all the control.

Brenda, she never spoke to Brenda. She didn't want me to see the truth. And the dream, she just accepted it, never questioned it. All thoughts are firing through my brain, the truth is clicking into place. I can't believe I was so stupid. How did I not realise?

I look around the room, there is nothing holding me to the bed. I'm not on a drip, there isn't a heart monitor. I see a bag underneath the chair Connor was sitting on. Perfect. I stand up and walk to the bag, opening it to see that Connor has packed me a small hospital bag. There are some clothes and toiletries in there. This is all I need. I quickly zip up the bag and put it over my shoulder.

Time to disappear again.

Thank you for reading!

Any support you can give to lift my book off the ground would be massively appreciated!

Sophie x

P.S I really hope Gracie got everything she was looking for and deserved...

@sophiesproof

@sophietat3

Printed in Great Britain
by Amazon

80146301R00173